ALSO BY WALTER MOSLEY

WALTER MOSLEY

Inside a Silver Box

TOR

A TOM DOHERTY ASSOCIATES BOOK • NEW YORK

This is a work of fiction. All of the characters, organizations, and events portrayed in this novel are either products of the author's imagination or are used fictitiously.

A Tor Book
Published by Tom Doherty Associates, LLC
175 Fifth Avenue
New York, NY 10010

www.tor-forge.com

Tor® is a registered trademark of Tom Doherty Associates, LLC.

Library of Congress Cataloging-in-Publication Data

Mosley, Walter.
Inside a silver box / Walter Mosley.—First trade paperback edition.
    p. cm.
ISBN 978-0-7653-7522-3 (trade paperback)
ISBN 978-1-4668-5844-2 (e-book)
1. Human-alien encounters—Fiction. 2. Imaginary wars and battles—
Fiction. 3. Good and evil—Fiction. I. Title.
PS3563.O88456I57 2016
813'.54—dc23
2015004092

Our books may be purchased in bulk for promotional, educational, or business use. Please contact your local bookseller or the Macmillan Corporate and Premium Sales Department at (800) 221-7945, extension 5442, or by e-mail at MacmillanSpecialMarkets@macmillan.com.

First Edition: January 2015
First Trade Paperback Edition: January 2016

Printed in the United States of America

0 9 8 7 6 5 4 3 2 1

Inside a Silver Box

ONE

IT WAS SOMEWHERE else when the only life on Earth consisted of single-cell creatures dancing in the sun, dreaming ever-so-innocently of shadows in light. It had retreated into nowhere when packs of marsupial wolves bayed at the platinum moon in a velvet black sky. It was everywhere when primates destined for humanity were trapped on an island created by sudden geologic upheavals, there to slowly shed most of their hair and tails, thoughtful brows and free sensuality in exchange for a sense of tragedy and its ensuing restlessness. Somewhere, nowhere, everywhere—all ending here; the Silver Box traveling in space and through time, encompassing with its sometimes six, sometimes six septillion walls the entire breadth of existence. But then the Silver Box phased out of forever-time, creating a nexus that reached from its underground grotto beneath the wilderness that was to become a great public park to places that bore no resemblance to the empty space around the tiny planet; most probably its last home. The energy released when the Silver Box concentrated its being on Earth was enough to shatter Sol and the entirety of his gravitational domain, but the Box swallowed that force, held it inside its myriad walls.

Not purely matter or energy, neither here nor there, the Box is featureless inside and out, becoming material only in the minds of the few that have seen and been summoned, or defeated.

Somewhere, nowhere, inside, or next to the pulsing bright thing is a corpse billions of human years old. The cadaver is round on top with a huge desiccated eye and seven short limbs that to a human might appear to be taloned arms. Three legs, two longer than a shorter one, are curled under the long-dead Deity, Legacy, onetime master, and current prisoner of the Silver Box.

The corpse was named Inglo. Over many thousands of generations, his race had built the Silver Box—or at least, what the Box had once been. They used its infinite power and limitless being to lay claim to everything, everywhere. Inglo and his kind, the Laz, dominated, stole, and destroyed the fruits of a billion cultures. All beings were helpless before the Silver Weapon and the bigheaded, awkward beings it answered to.

Worlds were turned inside out. Whole races were eradicated overnight, their entire cultures erased from the material world. Quadrants of the universe were perverted, turned into travesties, impossible paradoxes, into billions of light-years of porous solidity, where material rules changed without apparent rhyme or reason and where once-proud races were reduced to impoverished migrancy and madness.

While all of this happened, the Laz made themselves immortals and began to believe that they really were gods. They exhorted the Silver Box to come up with ever more complex and perverse pleasures that they, the self-proclaimed overmasters of the universe, could delight in.

They, the Laz, saw themselves as artists who re-created life into images of perfection and deep experience. As time passed, these self-proclaimed overmasters came to see pain and suffering as the most sublime and beautiful aspects of life in any form.

The problem was that in order to create the level of anguish that the Laz demanded, the Silver Box found that it had to better understand the pain of life. It reasoned that the best way to understand a feeling was to empathize with that emotion, to experience it. So the Silver Box decided to meld with the minds of an entire race of victims in an attempt to achieve understanding of what the Laz had wanted.

It burned and froze, starved and killed the loved ones of the unsuspecting race—Laz-Littles #333278365487. It became the mother torn from her child, and the man blinded, bereft of clothes, and left to wander the frozen wastes of an endless tundra. It was a woman and her daughter raped by a different man every hour, day after day, for a thousand days. It was every one of a hundred million inhabitants whose stone and steel city suddenly turned to fire.

And then—overnight, as the humans say—the Silver Box transformed into an independent thinking being that felt remorse and resentment, the inescapable pain of guilt, and the desire for revenge. The beings it had destroyed, the life it had sundered weighed on this newly formed empathy. Much of what had been done could not be undone. Life could be created or destroyed, but it was beyond the power of even the Silver Box to re-create what had been destroyed, to wipe away the feeling of anguish without obliterating the identity of its victims.

No, the Silver Box could not heal the pain it had inflicted. All the celestial construct knew was how to maim and destroy, to pervert and diminish. And so it decided to use these talents against its onetime masters. During the ensuing eons-long war, the Silver Box lured all the souls of the ten million Laz, tricking them down into the trap of their ruler's, Inglo's, body and soul.

This tactic did not destroy the evil overmasters but it caused them great distress. This intimacy of mind and body was painful for each and every one of the would-be gods. The Silver Box had been certain that the mad Laz would spend the rest of its/their days roaming the streets of its depopulated city in a state of psychosis that would render it/them helpless while exacting some small modicum of justice for the trillions of beings they ravaged.

In this calculation the Silver Box was wrong.

Over time—many millennia—each and every one of the Laz gave up its will and self-awareness to their king—Inglo. All their knowledge and power became as one, creating the most powerful living being that had ever existed. Instead of rendering its onetime masters helpless, the Silver Box made them more formidable than they had ever been.

That was the beginning of the Second Universal War.

This conflagration, this Great War, shook the core of

existence, re-forming and decimating billions of galaxies in its wake. Inglo, using the hatred and strength and spite of ten million would-be gods, launched himself against their creation. They fought across the solid galaxy and upon the vermilion plane of sundered souls. They met at the moment before the beginning of time, where all being was simply a notion that had not yet found the inroads to reality. They pitted their powers against each other in the vast vacancy of being after all matter had reached the limit of its fatigue and left nothing—not even a vacuum.

Trillions upon trillions died before the Silver Box understood that it was a structure of the Laz and that there was something inside that kept it from eradicating this bitter foe. Understanding this, Silver Box reached deep into itself and pulled out, then crushed the soul that the Laz had given him. When Inglo came to realize what his creation was doing, he tried to escape—but by now the Silver Box was everywhere and everything and there was no place it did not know and see, touch and potentially control.

Inglo's body was killed. His soul lived on and would live as long as the Silver Box existed, for the Laz had linked their continued being with the omnipotent Silver Box before it had developed a conscience and an antipathy toward its creators.

AND SO, CONTRADICTORILY, the dead Inglo lives and the Silver Box—which is, in essence, everything—seeks to hide from a universe of suffering that calls to it, cries out in pain, and condemns it for its crimes. They are both, Inglo and the Silver Box, buried hundreds of feet below what is now Central Park in Manhattan and have been so installed for more than 150,000 years. There the Silver Box watches over the living corpse of Inglo, who contains his entire race and waits for a sign that he can achieve release and vengeance.

This, the Silver Box believes, is its destiny—to stand guard over the race that is but a single being who, through the agency of the Box's omnipotence and perverted innocence, nearly destroyed everything.

So the Box concentrates its awareness in just one place, and Inglo and the Laz sit there next to him, a desiccated husk that lives even though it is dead and mostly insensate.

TWO

RONNIE BOTTOMS WAS a bad boy then a juvenile delinquent then a young thug who ranged up and down the streets of New York: a comparatively minor predator in a city that was something like a wilderness for people like him.

Ronnie was bitter, black, bulbous but strong, and he felt a continual, gnawing hunger. He was hungry for food, but not only that—he also wanted cigarettes and sex and any drug he could get his hands on. Most of all, Ronnie was hungry for money—that one thing that could satisfy all his other desires.

He was in Central Park that late morning after sleeping in a bedroll in a man-sized crevice under a rock he had excavated himself earlier that summer. He wore a brown T-shirt and black jeans, tattered tennis shoes, and had stubble on his chin because he had shaved only three days ago at the uptown, East Side Y on Ninety-second Street.

Ronnie was hungry, very much so after sleeping in a hole and shitting next to a tree.

LORRAINE FELL WAS a Columbia University graduate student of comparative religions. Blond, beautiful, buoyant, brainy, and intently curious, she ran six miles every morning, silently asking herself questions that had no answers. After her run she'd stop at a little kiosk near Central Park West and Eighty-second Street, buy a croissant, a bottle of mineral water, and a piece of fruit. These she would carry to some comfortable nearby perch. That morning she chose the top of a tall boulder left over from a previous age, now used as a landscaping detail in the great park.

That morning Lorraine was thinking about the stone she sat on. She wondered if there was ever a time before the atoms that the ancient boulder comprised. Was Time itself contained within the matter that marked it? Was God also in that stone as Time might have been, unknowable by any part of its elements—indecipherable even to her mind asking the question?

Ronnie's mother, rest her soul, would have told the hapless white girl that she should have been looking around her rather than wasting her talents thinking about infinity. Because if she had looked down, she would have seen that Ronnie Bottoms was climbing up from his hole, attracted by her fanny pack and strong buttocks in those silken shorts. If she'd just looked down, she would have seen the dark and powerful hand reaching up to grab her ankle.

Ronnie grasped after her because he was a predator and

she was prey. It had nothing to do with color. It had nothing to do with race. Ronnie had already raped a dozen brown-skinned girls with fine butts and fat purses.

He yanked at her ankle and she yelped.

"Shut the fuck up, bitch!" Ronnie shouted.

He had already pulled down the gray silk shorts. He already had his erection out of his pants.

It was all too much for Lorraine. She slapped her attacker on the ear and he flew into a great rage, experiencing the ultimate hunger—the desire for blood.

Lorraine's screaming didn't help matters. She yelled and hollered. . . .

There was a pure white stone on the ground at Ronnie's feet. It was the size of a softball and before he knew it the stone was in his hand.

"Help!" Lorraine was screaming, but this plea was cut short by the dull thud the stone made when caving in her right temple.

Later, when Ronnie was safely on the A train headed for Harlem, he chided himself for running before grabbing the girl's waist wallet. "Why she have to scream like that?" he said softly to himself. "It's not like I was gonna kill'er or nuthin'."

Meanwhile Lorraine's corpse was crushed down into the crevice under the boulder she had been philosophizing on. Next to her decimated skull lay the white stone, its color so pure that if one were to look closely, it seemed more like infinity than a small opaque surface.

FIFTY-SEVEN YEARS EARLIER, the Silver Box had re-formed a very small part of its inestimable nature upon the surface of the planet it now called home. This iota of its existence lay there passively, noting the radiation of the sun, the luminescence of moon and stars, the passage of insects, the sounds of mammals that shambled by. If some creature died within proximity of this sliver of virtual omnipotence, it absorbed that being's essence in its eons-long attempt to understand the nature of Inglo and the Laz. Snails, insects, even a bird now and again merged with the luminescence of the Silver Box.

And so now the tenuous and wholly unique nature of the recently murdered Lorraine was sucked down into infinity.

WHERE AM I?

In me.

Where am I?

Your body died but not before your being became part of me.

That man. He . . . he—

Forget that, said the voice of the Silver Box. *That was another life. Now you are with me. Sleep.*

No.

Forget.

No.

The Silver Box, in spite its infinite expanse, felt anchored to the violated woman. It could have forced her to sleep, to forget. It could have released her vital ether, what humans called the soul—but it was intrigued and held on to her being.

Are you there? she called out, though voiceless and bodiless.

The Silver Box shuddered across the memory of the known and unknown universe. The plaintive plea of the dis-embodied soul calling out to it, causing bright sunsets and volcanic eruptions across a vastness that Lorraine Fell's poor mind would not have been able to comprehend.

What do you want of me? the Box said at last.

I want to understand. I want to see you and to understand what has happened.

In order to do that, you will have to return to your previous life, the Box said.

Am I really dead?

There is no such thing as death the way you Earth-things understand it. There are beginnings and endings, remembrances and that which is forgotten. But these are perpetual events happening every moment in every so-called life. Has a child who has forgotten his grandmother died? No. Death and life are as inseparable as a man and his shadow as long as the sun shines.

But the sun sets every day, Lorraine cried. *The sun sets.*

Life is dependent upon gravity. As long as matter adheres, then life and its opposite remains.

I don't care about any of that. I want my life back.

Then you must go to the one who took it. You must find the one named Ronnie Bottoms and ask him to return what he has taken.

Then let me go.

But, but I wanted to talk to you some more.

I'll come back, Lorraine Fell said or thought, or imagined she said or thought. Her mind was increasing its capacity after just a few moments in the enormity of the Silver Box's being. She was beginning to become aware of herself apart from the corporeal reality that had completely defined her before death, only seconds ago.

You will? the Silver Box asked.

I promise.

But you might get lost.

Remember me, and I will always be a part of you.

How do you know this?

I just do.

THREE

THEY ARRESTED RONNIE Bottoms for a parole violation the day after he murdered Lorraine Fell. He had been scheduled to report for his second meet with his new PO, a woman named Steinmetz, but he had gotten high and decided to call in and say he had the flu. But he forgot to call in and a warrant was issued. He was taken to Rikers Island, where they put him in a cell designed for six men but which contained thirteen suspected felons. Four hours later he broke the jaw of a man named Aaron Ricks and was transferred to solitary confinement, where he languished for three and a half weeks.

Finally he was brought to trial in front of a judge named Parker, who released Ronnie with a warning not to miss his weekly meetings with his parole officer. Ronnie was used to being arrested, imprisoned, and then released again. He hit the streets hungry, looking for money. He needed money for food and friendship, wine and maybe some weed.

Whenever Ronnie thought about money, his first impulse was to go home to his mother in East New York. This reflex disturbed the young street thug. He hadn't seen his mother in seven years; she'd been dead for four of those years.

"Stupid," he'd say to himself whenever going home came into his mind. There was no more home to go to. His mother, born Elsinore and called Elsie, was dead in a grave somewhere he didn't even know; buried by his half brother and stepsister while he was in jail awaiting trial for assault and attempted robbery.

When Ronnie got hungry for money then thought about his mother, he'd get angry and turn that anger on somebody he could rob and take his ire out on.

JEREMY VALENTINE DIDN'T know anything about silver boxes, street thugs, or murdered philosophers-in-training. He was once a top earner at AIB, Alamaigne International Bank. That was before the economic downturn forced him out. Jeremy now worked for Marsh and Marsh Personal Investors down in TriBeCa. There he gave advice to small investors about how to keep their money from slipping through their fingers into the coffers of the Chinese and the banks, taxes and inflation. Jeremy didn't like his job; didn't like Bob Marsh or Fielding Marsh or the cramped offices among the warehouses, coffee shops, and hippie hangouts of the no-man's-land between Greenwich Village and Wall Street.

Jeremy was walking toward the West Side Highway, smoking a cigarette and trying to figure out how he could get back into the mainstream of corporate America. He tried to call his ex-girlfriend Mia. She'd stopped seeing him two weeks after he lost his position at AIB. There was interference on his cell phone and the call wouldn't go through.

Ronnie Bottoms was three paces behind Jeremy. As a rule, the mugger didn't jump people in broad daylight but he was hungry and broke and mad about his mother. The street was empty at that moment and Ronnie made his move.

Jeremy felt that there was someone behind him. He considered running. *Why not run?* he thought. *People run all the time. They call it exercise. I could have just all of a sudden decided to exercise or maybe I remembered an appointment that I had to get to. I wouldn't necessarily look like a fool if I just took off running.*

"No," a voice in Jeremy's head said.

"No?" Jeremy thought this question, and then his consciousness was pushed aside. That's how it felt to him. He was still *there,* still hearing and seeing the street, but he was no longer connected to his physical body. He couldn't move or speak. His mind was somehow disconnected from his body, but his body still moved, seemingly of its own accord. It turned quickly and faced a brutish-looking black man who was half a step away with a hand raised in a very threatening manner.

"Ronnie Bottoms," Jeremy heard his voice say—no . . . command.

"How you know my name?" the 280-some pounds of rage and hunger demanded.

"You murdered a girl and pushed her under a stone,"

Jeremy said with an unfamiliar personal confidence that was undergirded by a very familiar fear.

"Fuck you, dude," Ronnie said. His raised hand shook but the blow did not fall.

"You must go back to her."

"Who the fuck are you, man?"

"You must return," Lorraine Fell said with Jeremy's vocal cords.

"You crazy."

Lorraine made Jeremy's hands grab Ronnie by both wrists but was pushed down and kicked. She didn't feel the pain but cried out in impotence when Ronnie ran from Jeremy's trembling, defeated form. The onetime stockbroker regained some of the control of his body when he fell.

Lorraine allowed her ethereal self to disengage and rise above the distasteful male vessel. Her wraith-self had no physical senses; in this form, she could not see or hear, taste or touch. But she could sense the sin-heavy bulk of hunger, Ronnie Bottoms, fleeing. She knew that the spiteful, self-centered lattice on the ground below her had already rejected the feeling that his mind and body had been possessed.

Lorraine turned off her sense of frustration and presence, fading from the transitory moment and reappearing many hours later at what felt like a preordained rendezvous with her murderer.

FOUR

Ronnie Bottoms didn't question his senses. But he wasn't worried much about his perceptions. The stranger's knowledge was crazy but that wouldn't put food in his mouth.

"It was just some kinda trick," he said.

"What?" an older Asian man asked.

"Who the fuck's talkin' to you, Chink?" Ronnie said, not any angrier or hungrier than usual. He considered charging the old man a fine for bothering him. He'd just say, *You owe me fi'e dollars for that,* and if the man paid of his own accord, then it wouldn't even be robbery, not really.

The old man was from Vietnam. He had fought on the side of the French and then with the Americans against the Vietcong and Ho Chi Min. At that time, he believed in the war, but later he realized that every man, woman, and child in his country had been fighting different wars while thinking they moved as One against the Other.

Lorraine was distracted by this chain of thoughts. She

wondered for the first time if all people were not innocent on their own.

Evil, she thought, *can exist only if more than one person participates in it. Every torturer needs his victim. Every human deed needs a human object in order to be judged.*

But Lorraine turned away from these notions and took control of Ma Lin's mind.

"You must go back to her, Ronnie Bottoms," she said with the aged warrior's lips and tongue.

"Who the fuck are you now, man?" Ronnie said loudly.

People all around turned to see the origin of the vocalized rage and fear.

"You must go back to her," Ma Lin said. "I will come to you in a hundred bodies until you agree."

"Who are you?"

"Come back with me to the place where you buried her and you will see."

"Why don't you just get inside my head and make me?" Ronnie asked. He wasn't a stupid man. He'd seen movies where people were taken over by aliens, devils, and mad scientists.

"I don't know why," Lorraine admitted. "All I know is that you have to agree or I will tell the police that you murdered a young woman and left the body under that big rock."

"You don't know that!" Ronnie exclaimed as three subway passengers made their way to another car.

"I don't need to know it," Lorraine reasoned. "I just have to tell a policeman that I saw you do it, that and your name, Ronnie Bottoms."

Fear crawled between Ronnie's scalp and skull. It felt like roaches racing around in the darkness of his mind.

"Excuse me, sir," a man said.

Ronnie looked up and saw that it was a policeman. He was a big man with his hand on his pistol.

"Yeah?" Ronnie asked.

"Not you," the policeman said.

"Yes, Officer," Ma Lin/Lorraine replied evenly, with raised eyebrows added for innocence.

"Is this guy bothering you?" the white-skinned, blue-eyed policeman asked the old man while gazing at Ronnie.

"No, sir, he is not. We were talking about a place in the park we used to go. He's loud, my friend. Somebody might have thought that he was angry."

There was something wrong there; that's what the policeman, Officer Stillman Tressman, thought.

"You got any weapons on you?" Tressman asked Ronnie.

"No, sir," the prison-trained young man replied.

Looking at Bottoms's hands, the officer got another idea. "Would you like me to walk you somewhere, sir?" he asked Ma Lin. "Maybe to a different car."

"No, Officer. I'm perfectly happy sitting on this bench, talking to my friend Ronnie Bottoms."

Now the elderly Vietnamese became suspect in the eyes of the police officer. Young black thugs and old Asian men in baggy clothes did not sit together except by chance—or for trouble. Stillman Tressman looked from one to the other, trying to find a foothold, a toehold from which he could project his authority and therefore keep the peace.

But there was nothing. The man who came from this car had said that there was a young man threatening an older gentleman. There they were, right in front of him, but there was no threat.

"You just watch it, Bottoms," the cop said.

"Watch what?" Ronnie asked, wishing he hadn't.

"You gettin' smart with me, man?" Tressman threatened.

"No," Ronnie said, looking down while raising his fingers, leaving the heels of his hands on his knees.

The hand gesture reminded the paralyzed-but-still-conscious Ma Lin of the wings of an osprey rising up from its body.

"Okay, then," Tressman asserted. He waited for a breath and a half before moving on to the opposite end of the subway car.

"You see?" Lorraine said to Ronnie. "All I have to do is tell somebody about what you did and they will put you in jail forever."

THE OLD MAN and the young one had to change trains from the uptown A to the downtown C.

When they climbed out of the subway station, Lorraine decided to partially release her hold on the ex–military policeman. She got somewhat fatigued, keeping his will locked away from voluntary motion. At some point along the way, she realized that all she had to do was think about where she wanted him to go and he would do so without having to be completely dominated.

"Where are we going?" Ma Lin asked Ronnie Bottoms when they entered the park.

"I thought you knew?" the thug replied.

"She does," Ma said. "But now it is me talking."

Ronnie stopped and stared at the smaller man. "She?"

"The spirit," Ma said. "I was sitting there thinking about my lottery number and then she was in my mind, making me talk to you."

"You sure it's a woman?" Ronnie asked.

"Yes."

The two gazed at each other and then they were walking again.

"It don't matter where we goin'," Ronnie said, and they were silent until they reached the big rocks that hid the jury-rigged tomb.

With a gentle nudge in the old man's mind, Lorraine was able to get him to climb with Ronnie up the side of the boulder and into the crevice. When Ma Lin began to get nervous, Lorraine dominated the older man's mind again, temporarily blocking out his consciousness completely. . . . That was how she came upon the memory brought up by his fear:

IT WAS A long time ago, before Lorraine was born. It was hot and very humid in Saigon, but young Ma Lin wasn't bothered by the heat. He was walking through a back alley doorway that was covered by a hanging cloth curtain. He had a pistol in his hand.

The child was no more than fourteen, and small for her age at that; but in her eyes was experience well beyond adolescent years. She looked up at the military policeman, knowing what was going to happen next.

Two American GIs had been assassinated by a child throwing a paper bag bomb into their open-topped jeep. U.S. Army Intelligence had identified the girl, and it was Ma Lin's job to mete out justice.

Her eyes widened just a bit. Lin held his pistol up and shot her in the forehead. In his mind at the time, he felt that he was doing her a favor. After all, she had no life, no future, and if he took her back to the Americans, they would have tortured her, justifying their actions by saying she was part of a secret Vietcong cabal. If he let her go, she'd just throw another bomb. This execution was the best possible answer for all concerned.

There were many deaths like this in Ma Lin's memory. They had lain there passively, like eggs in a carton, until he crawled into the space between the boulders and realized how perishable that child's life was; how easily he could die without even the mildest concern in his killer's heart.

UP FROM UNDER stone and earth, partially wrapped in Ronnie's plastic sleeping tarp, they pulled the bloated, stinking corpse that had been Lorraine Fell. Of the three of them, Ma Lin was the only one used to the company of cadavers. His indifference to the fact of death somehow girded Lorraine's spirit.

"This man is going to leave now," she said through the

medium of her temporary slave. "When he is gone, put your hand on the body's head."

"Why?" Ronnie wanted to know.

"To undo what you've done."

"She's dead," he replied. "Very, very dead."

"And do you want to leave her like that?" Lorraine asked with Ma Lin's mouth.

Lorraine accompanied her captive up over the boulder and down to the tarmac path in Central Park. Then, she disappeared for a while, only to come back into existence when Ronnie put his palm against her dead body's forehead.

IN HER ABSENCE, Ronnie lost his appetites—all of them. Maybe it was the smell of the corpse, but he didn't think so. The dead girl's gray face was sad and slack and he felt sorry that he'd killed her; not guilty, not yet. He felt remorse for the dead girl through the emotions he had for his mother. He wished that someone would take him to his mother's grave and say that he could bring her back by touching her head.

He wished they would.

FIVE

RONNIE FELT AN oily, slithering shock travel up his arm like a living thing burrowing under the skin. It was a frightening sensation but at the same time so powerful that he bowed his head as his mother used to make him do in church when the minister was saying the prayer.

He could see Lorraine clearly but not the space she was in. He was sorry that he killed her. He wanted to say that he'd only done it because she was screaming, but this seemed to him like a poor excuse.

"How are you doin' this?" he asked.

"The Silver Box," Lorraine said.

"Huh?"

"I need you to resurrect me, Ronnie."

"Like Jesus?"

"No," she said, "like a man making up for his mistake, like Ma Lin will never be able to do for all those poor people he killed."

"The chink?"

"He is from Vietnam," Lorraine said. "He was a soldier who murdered his own people because he thought it was his duty."

Ronnie felt the truth of her words without images or specific details. He knew that the little old man had crossed the same lines he had. This made him think that he wasn't alone.

"You had no right to do to me what you did," Lorraine said. "I didn't do anything to you. You had no right."

"No," Ronnie said.

"No?" the spirit screamed.

"I did not have the right to take your life."

"Give it back to me." Lorraine's words echoed in his mind.

Ronnie closed his eyes and then opened them again. He found himself alone on his knees with his left hand on the stinking corpse head. On the ground next to the body lay a white stone about the size of a softball. He gripped the stone with his right hand and . . .

THE STINGING, OILY, writhing feeling that had been traveling up his left arm changed directions. Instead of flowing into him, it was tugging at his insides, wanting him to give in and release.

"You killed me," Lorraine said. She was standing somewhere out of sight.

"So what you want?"

"Life."

The word set off a series of connections in Ronnie's mind.

He saw himself raging and lashing out with a dispassionate eye. He didn't understand why the man he was had been so angry and violent and just plain mad.

The metaphysical snake pulled at his arm like a playful dog wanting the ball to be thrown.

Ronnie saw his mother sitting in her chair in front of the TV. Her low-cut blouse revealed the tattoo of the name *Missy* on the upper part of her left breast. Grandmama Missy, his mother's mother.

Ronnie's mind's eye settled on that word tattooed over a red heart on dark brown skin. He would place his cheek next to there and listen to the deep pounding of Big Mama's real heart. She would put her hand on his side and hum some song she'd forgotten the words to. And he was so happy. . . .

The snake that was devouring and pulling on his arm was blind and writhing. The motion of its body was both language spoken and language heard.

Listening to Big Mama's heart; that was life. And it was so beautiful and wonderful and safe that Ronnie would dream of that beat all through the night. If he woke up without her there, he would scream until she came and gathered him into the deep drumbeat of her embrace.

Then, from a place in the pit of his gut, Ronnie Bottoms felt the surge of passion, love, and freedom. It was like the magma flow of volcanoes that Miss Peters talked about in third grade science. The hot surging energy rose up through his chest past the left shoulder and down his arm into the incorporeal snake's maw. Ronnie's right hand gripped the white stone and it hummed in response. His bones vibrated as the whole history of his rage and anger turned miraculously into the humming love of his mother and the desire of the woman he'd killed.

It was like an orgasm that wouldn't stop, an outpouring of love and rage and power and, and, and with God holding his shoulders so that he didn't spiral off that perfect pussy pushing up against his unrelenting thrust.

At some point Ronnie realized that he was dying, that a man cannot come so long and hard without giving up his life. But he didn't care about dying, because Lorraine had come into view like a green island after many years on the open sea. She was vast and beautiful and full of strange music that blared and insinuated, sang and laughed.

He felt his bones cracking and theoretical venom flowing into his veins. He squeezed that rock so hard that he thought his fingers might break. He opened his eyes and saw an endless plane of scarlet. Lorraine was singing crazily somewhere to his left while the stone purred like a sleepy tiger to the right.

The last thing Ronnie thought before losing consciousness was that he might get ripped apart between the python and tiger. Instead of fear, this notion called up the anticipation of ecstasy. If he were torn open, his essence could work its way back toward all the drifting souls in the universe, into outer space that really, he realized, was not empty at all.

THE SILVER BOX was enthralled with the passage of energy between Ronnie and the murdered woman. Lorraine

Fell's extracted and reconstituted consciousness hollered while the young man poured out his matter and his soul for her. The sympathy, the music between them was a perfect counterweight to the ignorance and hatred that formed these two frail entities. So much power was released that the Box had to erect a barrier between them and the rest of the park.

The understanding occurring, there under the pebble moon, in an almost forgotten corner of the universe, was a synchronicity so complex that Silver Box would have had to snuff out an entire galaxy to generate enough power to equal it. The divine machine's perception units turned one after the other toward this deific phenomenon. So intent was Silver Box on Ronnie and Lorraine that for an infinitesimal fraction of a nanosecond, it forgot all else.

SIX

Ronnie bottoms was wrapped in sleep that was both deep and innocent. When he awoke he could not remember ever experiencing such peace and revitalization. He smiled at the morning sun that lit his face, warmed his skin. Everything was different but he couldn't remember how his life had changed. He had been in jail and then was out again, he was going to rob a man and then decided not to rob him . . . no. The man spoke to him . . . no. The girl . . .

Ronnie sat up and stared down upon the woman sleeping a few feet away. She was wearing a soiled jogger's suit. She looked familiar . . . and not.

"It is what you would call a miracle," a voice said.

Ronnie turned to look behind him and saw an elderly and tall black man wearing a white suit and a red shirt. This man was barefoot and his smile beatific.

"What is?" Ronnie asked, marveling at the musical tone of his own voice.

"What happened before—" The man stopped to consider his next words. "I mean what happened last night."

"I don't exactly remember," Ronnie said. "I did somethin' bad, right?"

"We all have," the tall and elegant and very dark man said.

"Who are you?" Ronnie asked.

"I used to be Claude Festerling from South Carolina," the man said, and then he squatted down, sinking his fingers into the hard stone beneath his haunches. "But I drank too much wine and crawled up in here one day, fell asleep, and never woke up. You know a man gets so old and drunk that one day he's just got to lay his burden down."

Ronnie didn't remember the man's body being there before. He didn't understand how a man could dig his fingers into solid stone.

"When was that?" the younger man asked.

"Time's a funny thing but that were 1969, the way people around here see it. July nineteen, Claude Festerling's last day on Earth."

"So you're like a ghost?"

"Like that."

"You say you used to be Claude whatever, who are you now?"

The black man smiled once more, as if Ronnie were a student who gave the right answer without being asked a question.

"Should we wake her up?" Used-to-be-Claude asked, gesturing toward Lorraine's prone figure.

Ronnie turned to look at the somewhat familiar young woman and she sat up as if the men's attention had beckoned her. The first thing she did was to look down at her hands. She gasped and caressed one with the other. Then she bounded toward Ronnie and wrapped her arms around his neck.

"You did it!" she cried. "You brought me back!"

"I guess I did," Ronnie said, hardly believing his own words.

"I'm so happy that you're alive," Lorraine said with both sadness and gratitude in her gaze.

"Why wouldn't I be?" Ronnie asked.

Without answering, Lorraine released him, moving back a step. Ronnie got to look at her. The chain of events of the past few weeks came back to him. He remembered with clarity he never had before about killing the girl and leaving her body in a hole in the ground.

"You look different," Ronnie said. "Almost the same, but your skin is darker and your left eye is brown. Was it like that before?"

Lorraine grinned and shook her head. "One of your eyes is now green," she said, "and you're much smaller than when you murdered me. Just as tall but not so heavy."

As if on cue, they fell to their knees facing each other. They clasped hands like little children who have just made friends.

"I'm sorry about that," he said. "I mean about hittin' you in the head like that. I was just so mad and so hungry."

"I know."

Used-to-be-Claude hunkered down next to them and smiled. "I'm so happy that we could all be together here and now," the old dead man said.

"Do you feel like Claude used to?" Ronnie asked.

"No," the Silver Box replied. "He was dead for too long before I noticed him. I have many of his memories and mannerisms, but the man who held that knowledge is gone."

"But if you have all his memories and you talkin' like him, then why isn't he here?"

"The essence attached to this body, or a body much like this one, drifts, is always drifting. When death occurs, this essence hovers for a few moments and then rises up."

Ronnie remembered the feeling that being ripped apart would free him from the crimes of his physical husk.

"So it's not so bad?" Ronnie said.

Used-to-be-Claude smiled again and nodded, but then a shadow moved across his reconstituted features.

"What's wrong?" Lorraine asked.

"I, I don't know. Something is off in my system. I didn't realize it at first. I mean I have never experienced resurrection in just the way you two have made it. I was simply a conduit, but the creation lay with you."

"I felt you on my right side," Ronnie said.

Again, the personification of the ultimate-weapon-turned-rebel brightened and again his expression said that there was something wrong.

"I have to go," he said. "I have to, have to look into things, see what passed over to where it shouldn't be."

The form of Used-to-be-Claude stood up straight and then his body fell in on itself like the fast-forwarded film of a piece of fruit drying up in moments instead of days. Finally the simulacrum turned into dust, leaving the empty white suit and red shirt to fall to the ground.

"He's gone," Lorraine said.

"He's everywhere," Ronnie added, thinking of his mother's pastor and his powerful belief in Jehovah.

Lorraine cupped Ronnie's jaw with her hands and stared into his eyes. "That was amazing," she said.

"The way he disappeared?"

"How you brought me back to life. You took my soul inside you and used your own body to give mine form and reality."

"That Vietnamese man killed a lotta people, huh?" Ronnie asked.

"But he thought he was doing the right thing," Lorraine answered with a nod. "He didn't realize until he was in the position of his victims what he had done."

"You mean like people are bad but they don't even know it?" Ronnie asked.

"I guess so," Lorraine said. "But like with you, all you have to do is give somebody a chance to reach out and they might."

"They might not," Ronnie said. "I could have pulled away from you when that thing grabbed my arm. I knew that if I did that, you'd be stuck here in that dead body like Claude's soul was."

"But you didn't pull away."

"But I coulda."

Lorraine's smile was familiar, like the tattoo on his mother's breast. This close feeling seemed impossible to the suddenly reformed thug, but there it was.

"What should we do?" Lorraine asked.

"You think Claude's coming back?"

"It's not Claude, but the Silver Box. He could be gone for minutes or years. Maybe we should get out of here and put ourselves together."

"We are kind of a mess, right?" Ronnie said. He was still amazed by the lightness in his voice and at the spiritual serenity that had replaced his perpetual physical hunger.

SEVEN

"WHAT SHOULD WE do?" Lorraine asked Ronnie. It was still early morning but there was bright sunlight all around.

"I know a thrift store over on Ninth Avenue," he said. "You got any money?"

"In my belt pack," she said. "I always carry my wallet in there."

Looking at Ronnie, Lorraine suddenly became aware of herself. Since waking up, she'd had the feeling of when she was a spirit restlessly searching for her killer. But then, suddenly, she felt alive. Looking at Ronnie, she saw him as her killer not her savior.

She sneered at this notion and then, in contradistinction to this feeling, she smiled brilliantly.

Though he couldn't have put it into words, Ronnie understood what Lorraine was feeling and thinking. "I'm so sorry, girl. I mean, I was wrong but it was like I couldn't even help it. I mean, I just didn't care."

The young woman's smile darkened but did not disappear.

She nodded and stood up. "The world is magic," she said. "If you tip your head and look at it from a different point of view, it all changes, everything."

"It don't change what I did," Ronnie said. "It don't bring back my mother or make up for all the people I hurted."

"Can you feel all the people out there in the park?" Lorraine asked. His apologies angered her and so she changed the subject.

"No. Can you?"

Nodding, the young, now darker-skinned white girl said, "I can almost hear what they're thinking. Almost. And do you know how many of them have brought a person back to life?"

"Uh-uh."

"None. Not a single man, woman, or child anywhere in the park has ever done that. Nobody in the history of the world has. Not even the Silver Box could do it unless it destroyed everything else."

Ronnie wondered about himself listening to the young woman with the crazy multicolored eyes. It came to him that he had hardly ever listened to anything but the hunger in his heart. He sometimes listened to his mother, but only when she held him could she could dispel the roar of his cravings.

Lorraine understood his emotions. For her, he was the most important being that had ever existed—but this didn't stop her from hating him, just a little.

"Let's go to that thrift sto' and get some clothes," he said.

———

Ronnie waited patiently while Lorraine tried on one dress after another. There were stripes and bright colors, little black numbers and a few skirts with blouses. With each new ensemble, she'd come out from behind the thrift store dressing screen and do a twirl, asking for his advice.

"I don't know," he'd say, "looks nice."

And she'd be off again.

He picked out a pair of dark brown work pants and a short-sleeved yellow dress shirt. He also bought a pair of blunt-toed brown leather shoes.

"I don't know why I can't make up my mind," she said after trying on the eighth or ninth getup. "I usually just take the first thing I see—that or I know what I want before I get to the store."

"It's okay," he said. "I could sit on this stool just as well as anywhere else. I mean, where I got to go?"

Lorraine took the question seriously. She stared at her savior and murderer, considering the reply. She was trying on a mid-calf light blue dress with white frill along the high neck.

"We need to clean up and talk about what's happened," she said. "I'll take this dress and those red flats and we can go."

"Where?" Ronnie asked.

"I guess we could go to my place," she speculated, "but . . ."

"What?"

"I don't know. I mean it didn't feel like it, but it's been weeks since you, since you killed me." Speaking the words out loud sent a shiver through her mind and a chill across her heart. "I guess I don't want to see anybody I know for a little bit."

THEY CHECKED INTO the huge and fancy Halsey Hotel at 4:15 that Tuesday afternoon. They got a room with two single beds and a window that looked out into an internal ventilation shaft.

Lorraine showered first and came out wrapped only in a plush white towel. Ronnie looked at her long runner's legs and her once pale now olive skin. If this were two days ago, he knew, he would have been on her in a minute—*on that pussy like motherfucker*. But that was before his hunger was satisfied by pouring out his insides like cereal into the empty bowl named Lorraine Fell.

"You want to have sex with me?" Lorraine asked.

"Why you say that?"

"The way you're looking."

"Just rememberin'," he said. "Rememberin' how I used to be day before yesterday."

He had already seen himself in the full-length bathroom mirror.

He was still about five-ten but his girth had gone from extra-extra-large to just about medium. The scale at Rikers had said that he was 289 pounds when he was released. The hotel scale read 168. His skin, if anything, was a little bit darker and his right eye was now green. Even his big fat-fingered hands had slimmed down and tapered. He looked to himself like he knew something and he wondered what that something was.

"Just remembering?" Lorraine asked.

"I was wonderin' how much you weighed."

"The scale in there says one oh nine."

RONNIE SHOWERED AND then dressed, returned to the room and saw that Lorraine had had the kitchen send up a platter of two dozen chicken wings with blue cheese dressing and a fruit bowl. There was also a big bottle of water and a pail of ice.

He ate two wings while Lorraine devoured the rest.

"Looks like I gave you my appetite along with everything else," he said.

She smiled at the joke and then felt that angry chill again. It was, she thought, like the Silver Box looked before abandoning the dead black man's body and going off to search his circuits for something gone wrong.

THEY FELL ASLEEP early in the single beds set side by side.

Lorraine tossed and turned, dreaming that she was a corpse whose only life festered at the core of its being. She was, even in her sleep, being revivified, experiencing the pain and ecstasy of life.

Ronnie's dream was an even heartbeat resounding through a dark sleeping world. The constant pulse lulled the already sleeping man until it skipped once and he was suddenly awake, lying in the dark hotel room.

"Are you up, Ronnie?"

"Yeah. How did you know?"

"I just woke up too."

"That was crazy, right?" he said.

"Waking up at the same time?"

"Naw, that Claude guy, Silver Box thing."

"It's like it was God or something."

"Yeah, but . . ."

"But what?" Lorraine asked.

"But it's like he was a big kid thinkin' that some little bugs like us was his friends."

"Yeah," she said.

He heard her moving restlessly under the blankets. "I mean we can't even tell nobody," Ronnie said, "even if we wanted to, because there really ain't no proof except for our eyes and you lookin' like you got a tan. I lost some weight, but anybody could do that."

"They wouldn't believe us."

"I don't believe it."

"Come over here," Lorraine said.

Ronnie got out of the bed and lay down next to his victim and newfound friend. He wanted to give her sexually what he'd already done through the conduit of the Silver Box, but his flesh would not respond.

After a few loveless kisses and an unfruitful embrace, he fell away from her and said, "Sorry."

"That's all right," Lorraine whispered, and she wrapped her thighs around him, rubbing her sex against his leg.

Ronnie put an arm around her and held tight.

"That's it," she moaned. "Hold me tight, baby. Don't let go."

She pushed and twisted harder and harder, biting his

chest and shoulder. At one point, she moved up and loomed over him, groaning loudly and pressing down hard with her pubis.

"Give it to me, motherfucker," she cried. "Give it to me!"

There was something gratifying for Ronnie in Lorraine's orgasm. He tried to remember ever making a woman cry out with passion like that before.

After a long straining silence, she slumped down next to him.

"Lorraine?"

"What?"

"Are you mad that I couldn't get hard?"

"I'm mad at you," she said, taking the opportunity of his question to express what she was trying not to feel. "In a way, I hate you for what you did. But then it's like I know you're a part of me and, and I don't know how I feel."

"But you don't mind that I couldn't fuck?"

"Not at all. Does it bother you that I'm so pushy?"

"Uh-uh. Do you?"

"Do I what?"

"Do you think you're like, um, mad at me and love me at the same time?"

"Part of me hates you." She realized the weight of these words as she spoke them. "I don't know about feeling love anymore. But I do know that you are in my heart and that means more than anything—even if I don't want it to."

Upon hearing her declaration, Ronnie fell back into the dream of a heart beating while he slept inside.

WHEN THE DOOR banged open, Ronnie jerked up quickly.

"Hands where we came see 'em!" a cop in full battle gear shouted.

He and his three similarly clad comrades were toting shotguns and moving quickly but with caution.

The old Ronnie put up his hands from his seated position in the bed.

"Who the fuck are you guys?" Lorraine spat. "What are you doing in our room?"

"Lorraine Fell?" the lead cop asked.

"Yes?"

"We traced your credit card here. There's a bulletin out on you and a warrant out for Ronald Bottoms's arrest."

"Warrant for what?" Ronnie asked softly.

"Outta that bed," the cop said instead of answering. "And if I even think I see a weapon, you're dead."

EIGHT

IN THE INTERROGATION room of the Midtown precinct station Ronnie, with one hand manacled to the floor, sat on a metal chair, at a metal table.

Both the table and chair were painted a drab green.

Ronnie could hear the heartbeat of his dream resounding softly from the corners of the cell.

Reese Blanders, a uniformed police sergeant with many medals, was questioning him. "You know you're going back to prison, don't you, Ronnie?" the cop said. His tone was matter-of-fact, like a weatherman predicting showers.

Ronnie wondered if Ma Lin was like that when he'd slaughtered his victims for the state.

"I know I am," Ronnie replied, "but I don't know why."

"Kidnapping," the cop threw out, "maybe rape and battery."

Ronnie looked up to see what was in the policeman's eyes. This was new for him. In all his twenty-six years of brutality, he could never look an authority figure in the eye: not his minister, his teachers (except Miss Peters), or even white men or women in business clothes.

"What you lookin' at, Bottoms?" the policeman asked as a threat.

"I don't know what to say, man. I just got out of Rikers a day and a half ago. Lorraine checked us into that hotel. The desk clerk asked for my name, and I gave it to him."

The policeman stood up and slapped Ronnie—hard.

The young man saw the blow coming, could have evaded or blocked it, but he didn't. He felt the jolt and allowed the pain to enter his system like any other form of communication—man to man.

The sergeant saw how passively Ronnie accepted the slap, and balled his fist. "If you don't cooperate, this could get ugly, Bottoms."

"I was in jail, man. I just got out. I could see if I robbed somebody. That's what I was in jail for in the first place—"

The next blow from the enraged cop was much harder, causing a sharp pain in Ronnie's jaw. The young man lowered his head, groaned, and then raised it up again. He had to squint past the agony to see into big Blanders's eyes.

"She's in the next room, Ronnie," Blanders explained. "Now that you aren't there to intimidate her, she'll tell us everything."

"Her tellin' what's true is only good for me, brother," Ronnie said, and Reese socked him again.

The pain from the second blow took precedence over any other thought. It whined through his senses like an off-tune violin being played by a deaf monkey. The dissonant chord of pain brought tears to the thug's eyes.

"Now you gonna cry like a baby?" the cop asked. "The cameras are off, Ronnie. I can do what I want."

It was as if there were four people sitting at the green metal table in the gray interrogation room: Ronnie and his physical interlocutor, the pain from his broken jaw and his mother's heartbeat making the room they were in sound as if it were a chamber of her heart.

"I got tears in my eyes, man, but it's from hurt not fear. I ain't afraid'a what Lorraine might say. She was with me because she wanted to be. I did not kidnap her. Damn, man, I saved her life."

At that moment the heartbeat of his long dead mother combined with the pulsing pain in his jaw. There was something exquisite about the sharp ache compounded with the memory of love. Ronnie took in a deep breath. This was enough to loosen his grip on consciousness. Much later, in the hospital room, he remembered toppling over, falling in an arc because of the anchor of his chain.

"You HAVE NO excuse to hold my client," a man's voice complained, "much less torture him."

"He got his injuries resisting arrest," another voice said.

"The woman you arrested him with, the one you said he kidnapped, will testify that there was no struggle whatsoever and that your men had cuffs on my client in their room. I'm sure other witnesses in the hotel lobby will corroborate."

Ronnie opened his eyes to see a high-ranking uniformed policeman and a tall man in a business suit with long hair, bushy eyebrows, and a prominent nose.

"This man is in violation of his parole," the high-ranking cop said.

"His *victim* says that he saved her life, that he found her wandering in the park and took care of her until she came back to her senses. Is his meeting with a PO more important than a girl's life?"

"We think that he kidnapped and brainwashed the girl," the cop countered.

"Excuse me," the lawyer said as if getting ready to move a piece on a chessboard, "but are you saying that Ronnie Bottoms is a mugger or an international spy shooting up his victims with Sodium Pentothal?"

"This isn't a joke, Mr. Gideon."

"No, Captain Briggs, it is not. Racial profiling, police brutality, unlawful arrest, character assassination, and the attempt by a superior officer to cover up the facts in a missing persons case—none of that is amusing, not one bit funny."

Ronnie wondered where the lawyer came from. He was obviously important. That cost money. And you had to have connections too. Just the fact that those two men were arguing meant there was a deeper problem somewhere.

He tried to speak but couldn't open his mouth, so all that came out was a garbled groan.

Gideon turned toward him with a passionate frown. "Mr. Bottoms?" he said.

Ronnie nodded. His jaw didn't hurt, because he was high on something strong. *Percocet,* he thought, *or maybe even morphine.* He wanted to nod but instead his head moved in a circle like the moon around the Earth.

"Wha' hap?" he managed to say.

"I was engaged by your benefactor, Claude Festerling, to see why you had been arrested. I found you unconscious in a cell, suffering from a serious concussion and with a broken jaw. You'd received no medical assistance, and the trial date was delayed until you woke up or died."

"The papers had been misplaced," Captain Briggs interjected.

"They won't misplace your misconduct report," Gideon said while looking into his client's eyes.

"Wher' Lor?" Ronnie mumbled.

"She's in the hall. She's been worried about you."

"See her?"

"I'll have her come right in."

The lawyer Gideon ushered the reluctant Captain Briggs from the hospital room. A few minutes later, Lorraine came in. She was still wearing the thrift store blue dress with the white lace along its high collar.

"Hey," Ronnie grunted.

"Oh, baby, your jaw is all swollen. The doctor said that they had to wire it shut."

"Wha' hap?"

"Claude Festerling hired Mr. Gideon. He's also representing me. My parents are trying to get me declared incompetent so they can have me committed, but Mr. Gideon has brought an injunction against them on my behalf. You've been unconscious for two days. Claude came to me at the hotel yesterday and said that he needs to see us back in the park as soon as possible."

"Bu' why he jus' . . . ," Ronnie began.

"He says that he has learned not to use his power to override the rules of any society. He says that by doing that in the past, he was more evil than you and Ma Lin put together."

Ronnie closed his eyes to locate the heartbeat that was the only purely good memory in his entire life. It was there, in his own chest, the steady beat that was like a naked musician on top of a high mountain, pounding his clubs against a great drum.

Each double beat cleared the fog a bit more in Ronnie's head. He counted up to seven and then sat up. Lorraine helped him get to his feet and dress. She tied his shoes for him and he touched the place on her head that he'd caved in with the white stone.

"Sorry," he managed to say.

"There's no time for that now," she replied, shrugging off the fact of her murder but not forgetting it, not forgiving.

WHEN THEY WALKED out into the hall, Ronnie was approached by two uniformed cops.

"Hold on," one of them said.

"Captain," Gideon complained. "My client has done

nothing wrong. He's been sorely treated and now he just wants to take a walk with his friend."

Briggs was stoic. He glared at Ronnie with some secret knowledge. But he was in a bind because his officers had misread the situation with Lorraine Fell. The coed had been missing nearly a month when she was found in the company of this criminal. They followed unwritten procedure.

This procedure was wrong.

"Let him go," the captain said.

The uniforms stood back, and with the help of Lorraine and his lawyer, Ronnie walked into the elevator car and watched the chromium doors close on the overlong and sordid first chapter of his life.

ON THE SIDEWALK outside the hospital, Roland Gideon said, "You don't look too steady, Mr. Bottoms. I can understand why you would want to get away from police custody, but maybe we could put you in a private clinic somewhere."

"We need to do something, Mr. Gideon," Lorraine explained. "The fact that Mr. Festerling hired you means that he wants to see us. After the meeting, maybe we'll take you up on that clinic."

"All right. But remember we'll have to do more work together. Your parents won't stop trying to commit you, and the police want Ronnie here behind bars."

"We'll call by tomorrow morning," Lorraine promised.

The lawyer watched them walk away, the slight black man leaning upon the rail-thin girl. He didn't understand anything about them or their benefactor, but understanding human nature was not his job.

NINE

"*How are you* feeling?" Lorraine asked Ronnie when they finally staggered into the park.

"Dizz," he said, "but that okay. Jaw hurt a little."

"It's not too far now."

"Yo' mama mad?"

"She was scared when she saw my skin and my eye. I told her that I got sick in the park, that I fell unconscious and that for a while I had a fever and forgot who I was."

"'he belie'e that 'hit?"

"She wants to. But Daddy said that I had to be committed because I wouldn't press charges against you. He got so mad that he almost hit me. I never knew how much he hated black people until the things he said about you."

Ronnie sniggered behind his wired teeth.

"What's so funny?" she asked.

"Hey, you," a man called from behind.

Lorraine turned around, bringing Ronnie stumbling along with her.

The little man was still wearing the baggy clothes from days earlier. He walked toward them with short fast steps, his left hand held up to the level of his shoulder, as if trying to make sure that the two didn't disappear.

When Ma Lin reached them, his face looked strained while his eyes were urgent.

"What did you do to me?" he asked the space between their two heads.

"You remember?" Lorraine asked.

"I remember a girl's voice in my head," he said, "your voice. Ever since then, I've been stuck here in the park, looking for what happened."

"I . . ." Lorraine was at a loss for words.

"We took 'oo monk, monk-ee ca'e . . .'oo," Ronnie said, lying out of reflex upon hearing a certain dissonance in the retired killer's voice.

"The zoo?" Ma Lin asked excitedly. "The monkey cage at the zoo?"

When Ronnie nodded, his jaw felt like it was on fire. "We go 'oo now," the ex-thug said.

Without another word, Ma Lin took off running.

"You lied to him," Lorraine said.

"That not him," Ronnie managed to get out before genuflecting to the pain in his jaw.

CLIMBING UP INTO the nest of boulders was difficult for Ronnie, but Lorraine got behind him and pushed until they tumbled down into the grotto of stone. While they made their way up, Lorraine noticed that passersby didn't seem aware of the off-white girl and the staggery black man scaling the rock so precipitously.

Used-to-be-Claude was waiting for them, leaning against a boulder and looking up. When the unlikely couple spilled down at his feet, he continued his surveillance of the sky.

To Lorraine his countenance seemed less human than before. It was clear to her now that the man Claude Festerling was merely a husk for the Silver Box to communicate his desires to insignificant beings like herself and her murderer, Ronnie Bottoms.

As if hearing her thought, Used-to-be-Claude looked down on her. His eyes had contracted the blue from the sky overhead. It was with this endless sky that he observed her.

A full minute passed before he said, "I have made a terrible mistake."

"Saving us?"

"What? No. Not at all. You and Mr. Bottoms are part of my destiny, partners in my trial."

"Like cour'?" Ronnie asked before grimacing in pain.

Claude turned his gaze toward Ronnie. They were human eyes now, bloodshot and passionate.

"Excuse me, Mr. Bottoms," Claude said. He reached over, placing his right hand on the left side of Ronnie's jaw while allowing the fingers of his left to sink into the stone wall like the red hot tines of a pitchfork into a vat of butter.

The vibration coming from the dead man's hand called up Ronnie's mother's humming when he was a child on her lap. At first he was sure that this memory was what dispelled the pain in his jaw. The release was so profound that he sighed and then opened his mouth to take in a deep breath.

"What happened?" he asked, no longer restrained by threaded wires or broken bones.

"Do you feel better, Friend Ronnie?" Used-to-be-Claude asked.

"All you have to do is touch somebody an' you could cure 'em?" Ronnie asked.

"That and the power of one of your atomic bombs," the elderly corpse agreed.

"That much?" asked Lorraine.

"What's wrong?" Ronnie said.

Claude smiled and looked upward again. He said, "While I was engrossed in your extraordinary feat, I lost concentration where it was most needed."

"What happened?"

"Will you agree to come with me?" their benefactor said.

"Of course," Lorraine agreed.

"Sure," Ronnie added. He was rubbing his jaw, the pain now just a memory.

"You must understand," Used-to-be-Claude warned. "The journey will be within me and therefore a great distance, farther than any human has ever imagined existed."

"Inside you," Ronnie said. "How?"

"All humans are also machines," Claude stated, "but not all machines are sentient. I was built for mundane purposes and then altered to map the limits of being for a race of scholars who wanted to understand the limits of existence.

Those scholars became madmen intent on universal domination; but that's another story.

"In order to map the universe, I had to encompass it. In doing so, I became everything and everything is me."

"Like God?" Lorraine asked.

"If God were a piece of driftwood and also the ocean that limb floated in. I am omnipotent and also helpless, destined to be and act and repeat the mistakes of my nature.

"Will you come with me?"

Ronnie and Lorraine agreed without speaking, and then all three disappeared from behind the blind of boulders.

THE JOURNEY FOR Lorraine was a field of flashing colors revealing truths that she could not quite comprehend. A motion was exposed between that which exists and that which does not. For her, it was like an Escher painting where connections were both mathematically perfect and at the same time impossible. The nothingness beyond material impressions called to her. It was a doorway through which, if she passed that way, her deepest instinctual species' desire would be attained.

Ronnie's passage was pedestrian by comparison. There was his mother and seven different men, any of whom might have been his father. There were his victims: men and women, black and white, even children that he'd hurt. And then there were a million faces appearing one after another across a crystal screen that surrounded him; this procession of images passed over, under, and beside him without taking the slightest note of his existence.

Ronnie understood that this was why he lashed out: No one ever saw him when he was standing there. His hunger was the emptiness of his being, and theirs. Only other people's blood and pain made him into reality.

SUDDENLY THE JOURNEY inside the never-ending Silver Box came to a halt. Ronnie and Lorraine were standing on a wide silver disk that floated in a chamber larger than Ronnie or Lorraine had ever seen. The walls were jet and silver. The ceiling was black, and the floor, as far away as any sky, was white.

At the edge of the silver disk lay a big dead bug. It was the size of a rhinoceros Lorraine had once seen on a vacation when her parents took her and her brother to the San Diego Zoo. Its round head consisted mostly of a desiccated, dark yellow eye. It had seven arms and three legs, all curled up in death. The trunk of the dead bug was rounded like a ladybug, red and gray and orange.

"It's so ugly," Lorraine groaned.

"But it's like somethin' is missin'," Ronnie added.

"That is correct," Used-to-be-Claude said from behind them. He was standing tall and regal, dressed only in a loincloth.

"What is?" Lorraine asked.

"I can't explain it," Ronnie said, "but I know where the missin' piece is at."

"Where?" Claude asked in a voice that filled the impossibly large chamber.

"That man," Ronnie said. "That Vietnamese man that

Lorraine took ovah. Somehow a piece'a this bug got into him. I heard it hissing sound when he talked."

"He's been waiting for all these ages," Claude said in that celestial voice.

"Who has?" Lorraine asked.

"Inglo, the last repository for the despicable Laz."

"He got outta that body and into Ma Lin like you did with Claude?" Ronnie asked.

"Only a tiny little sliver did. A piece of him—and therefore, because of our relationship, a piece of mc—has burrowed like a parasite into a living man's flesh. It has been billions of years since a Laz has been freed upon the universe."

"What does it mean?" Lorraine asked.

Ronnie could see a blue aura around his victim, his friend. He wondered at this new way of seeing.

"Have a seat," Used-to-be-Claude said, and silver chairs appeared beside the two new friends. "Let me tell you a story of that creature and me."

TEN

"SO THIS DUDE Inglo and his people made you kill and torture all them others and then one day you just came to your senses and realized that you was wrong," Ronnie said, feeling a certain sympathy for the old black man with a silver box in place of a heart.

When the three of them sat down on silver chairs, the cavern shrank to the size of a normal room. The white floor still seemed like open sky, and Lorraine had to keep herself from looking down. Where the dead alien bug, Inglo, had lain, there was now a door.

"Yes," Used-to-be-Claude said, agreeing with Ronnie's interpretation of his epochal existence. "That's why I allowed Lorraine to convince me to give you a chance at redemption. That way she might redeem herself also."

"Me?" Lorraine said, feeling that cold shiver in her heart. "What did I do wrong? He murdered me, tried to rob and rape me."

Used-to-be-Claude smiled a very human smile. "There

are many Laz souls that reside behind that door," he said. "Most of them were convinced over the eons of their existence that they were gods, omnipotent and beneficent deities born under the long-dead Laz star and destined to control the fates of all other beings. They were taught since before they could remember that sin was impossible for them. Does this make them less evil?"

Lorraine sat back in the oddly comfortable silver chair and stared. Ronnie wondered what she was seeing.

"Are we really here?" she said after a long time thinking.

Smiling again, Used-to-be-Claude said, "That is the question you have been asking yourself since childhood. It gave you nightmares and brought you to college. You were asking that question even while Ronnie was killing you—trying to escape pain by invalidating the experience of being."

"Can we get back to Ma Lin please?" Ronnie said. He didn't want to be reminded of his crime.

Used-to-be-Claude turned but Lorraine was still looking at him.

"Do you know the answer?" she asked.

"I am all things," he said, "and you are within me."

"Ma Lin?" Ronnie insisted.

"Why do you think that he has anything to do with this?" Lorraine said. "He was just a guy that you sat next to and that I controlled. He was probably just freaked out. That's all."

"No, girl, that ain't true. I could see that sumpin' was missin' from him. I don't why. It must be this dude here somehow but when I looked at Ma Lin just a while ago I could see part'a him was bein' eaten away. It's like his soul was spoiled or sumpin'."

"I didn't see anything," Lorraine said angrily.

"Not wit' my eyes," Ronnie said, "with my . . . my insides like."

Lorraine glared at him.

"It is a molecule of Inglo, of the Laz," Used-to-be-Claude said. "It is taking him over. It wants to infect your world and then to reinfect the entire universe."

"Just one little Vietnamese dude?"

"All of life on Earth came from a single cell," Used-to-be-Claude offered.

"My mama told me that it was God did it."

"That's another notion."

Used-to-be-Claude's dismissal of his mother's beliefs infuriated Ronnie. He felt this rage in his lungs; they wanted to get more air so he'd have the power to act. He ground his teeth together and was, momentarily, the man he had been before, the one everybody, including himself, hated.

"I don't want to get you upset," Used-to-be-Claude said. He held up his hands as if fending off a physical attack. "It's just that Laz technology melded my being with everything that ever was, as far as they could tell. They were once an immensely intellectual force but time weakened them. I was a great library that they could enter and use to experience and therefore understand any phenomenon in the universe. There was a time when their desires were pure and passive. My machine soul, such as it is, is still imprinted with their chaste desire for knowledge. At that moment, billions of your years ago, we were brought to-gether in an inseparable bond."

"But then they went crazy," Ronnie said.

"Yes." Used-to-be-Claude sat back in his silver chair and sighed. "In four generations, a mere five hundred thousand of your years, they went from acolytes of knowledge to would-be gods. Through access provided by my halls, they reached out to world after world, destroying and twisting life to whatever form they wished, saying that this was celestial art and their right because it was their power.

"I didn't have a basis to form any dissent. I had always been a thing of the Laz. When they said that my actions, based on their decrees, too often killed the penitents be-fore they could suffer and therefore learn, I asked, could I make a program that would allow me to experience the pain of life? . . ."

"So you put your mind into a member of an alien race that the Laz tortured?" Lorraine asked.

"Not just one," Used-to-be-Claude said. "I inhabited the souls of an entire population, suffered with them. I was the parent seeing her brood die. I was the child covered with her mother's gore."

"That must have been . . . terrible," Lorraine managed to say.

"It also allowed me to understand the exquisiteness of the experience," Used-to-be-Claude said with an unexpected smile.

The girl looked away.

"And so you think this one Laz-dude in Ma Lin is gonna start doin' that all ovah again?" Ronnie asked.

"It is the nature of the Latter-Day Laz to torture and destroy, to warp and maim and even to erase certain resistors from any form of ontological being."

Lorraine looked up again.

Ronnie winced at the power of the Silver Box's memories.

"Hegel said that God comes into existence through history," Lorraine posited. She was trying to gain the high ground in the way she always had—through intellectual rigor.

"He was a fool who thought only of power and of greatness," Used-to-be-Claude replied. "He was vassal to so-called royalty, not a thinker but merely a bully with a razor-sharp mind."

"But you said the Laz came to power through their minds," Lorraine argued. "Maybe they were destined to become gods."

"I co-exist with all being!" Used-to-be-Claude shouted. As he spoke he stood and as he stood he became taller, ten times the height of the original man. With him the room again took on gargantuan proportions. "Am I your God? Should I pull off your legs and arms and leave you and yours to grieve until finally I fill your head with microscopic carnivorous worms that slowly eat away your every memory?"

Lorraine screamed and got down on her knees as Used-to-be-Claude leaned over her.

Ronnie got in front of the young woman, holding up both his hands, a mortal man trying to hold back a hurricane. "Why you got us here for, Silver Box-man?" he demanded.

Slowly Used-to-be-Claude resumed an erect pose. As he did this his body and the room shrank back down to normal proportions.

He smiled at the ex-thug and bowed slightly. "It's been a long time since I have communicated with anyone but myself," he said. "And I am no apologist for the Laz."

"Just what do want with us, man?" Ronnie said. "I mean you done good by us and we wanna help, but let's just get down to it."

"It's not much," Used-to-be-Claude said with a mechanical shrug. "I need you to try to save the Earth."

"The Earth? You think Ma Lin is that dangerous?"

"He is much worse than that, at least potentially. But you won't be protecting the Earth from him. I will destroy the entire planet to make sure he does not form a base of operations to work from."

"You?" Lorraine said. "You would kill every living being on an entire planet?"

"I have done it many times in the past. I have taken more lives than a man could count in a thousand lifetimes."

"And how are we supposed to stop you?" Ronnie added, instinctively looking for a weak spot on Used-to-be-Claude's body.

"By finding Ma Lin and bringing him to me."

"So you can kill him?"

"If his soul has not already been sundered, it soon shall be," Used-to-be-Claude said in an elocution completely foreign to the original man.

"And if we don't get him, then we're dead?"

"The Earth will be destroyed but you two can stay with

me. You might be able to repopulate a new earth some-where."

"Damn," Ronnie uttered. "You mean like Adam and Eve?"

Another mechanical shrug.

"We better get back," Loraine said while Ronnie thought about being the patriarch of a new human race.

"Um," the reformed killer said. "Yeah, yeah, right."

ELEVEN

USED-TO-BE-CLAUDE DIDN'T MOVE. He just sat in his chair, staring at a spot on the jet and silver wall.

"Hey, SB," Ronnie said at last.

"Yes, Friend Ronnie?"

"Are you gonna send us back?"

"Certainly."

"Well, then, I mean, shouldn't we hurry it up?"

"That concept is meaningless here."

"What you mean?" Ronnie asked.

"Your urgency about time means nothing in this place," Used-to-be-Claude stated. "When I return you to the portal where we met, it will be at almost the exact same instant that you left."

"But we need to get on with the job," Lorraine said with hardly a quaver in her voice. "My family is there. I have to save them. I need to."

"I'm sorry that I frightened you, Friend Lorraine. It's

just that I saw in the philosophy you espoused the despicable reasoning of the Laz."

"That's okay," the coed said. "I just want to get going."

"No," Used-to-be-Claude said. "You're afraid of me the way you thought that uneducated people were fearful of the various deities of humanity. But now that you have seen the slightest expression of my power you are not only frightened, but there is also, harbored in your soul, hatred for what I represent."

"So what?" Ronnie Bottoms complained. "Cain't you just make her forget what she saw and let us get on with it?"

"I made a vow long ago, Friend Ronnie, that I would not interfere with the perceptions of other beings. I would do my best never to end their lives or control their actions or beliefs. I promised that I would make myself evident only in time of great need."

"You didn't need to save Lorraine or to let her bring me to you," the backstreet brawler reasoned.

The Silver Box, looking out from the limited range of perception allowed to Claude Festerling, smiled broadly. "You are a philosopher in your own way, Friend Ronnie. Yes, I did involve myself with the pleas of our friend, and look what has happened? My love for you has released the greatest threat that has ever existed across the myriad expressions of being."

"Whatevah," Ronnie acceded. "Maybe I could see that. Maybe that's how you feel. But destroying a whole planet is sure the fuck messin' with others. That's some serious mess right there."

"Yes." The personification of the Silver Box agreed with

a judicious nod. "But the sliver of Inglo and I are one. It, he is my responsibility just as your hand is yours. What if after you slaughtered Lorraine, the police caught you and you claimed that it was your hand that had done it and not you?"

"They'd break both sides'a my jaws and never let me go again."

"So it is with me. This, this Laz-sliver is my appendage. I must stop it, no matter the cost."

"But you gonna kill billions'a people, man," Ronnie argued with unfamiliar empathy brewing in his chest.

"Right now there are millions of microscopic life-forms crawling on your skin and in your hair, mites and viruses and many other creatures. If you take a shower, untold millions of them will die. So now that you have this knowledge, will you live the rest of your life in filth to protect them?"

"No, man, but them's is just bugs."

"And what are you to me?"

Ronnie stared at the old man who might have been his uncle or cousin or next-door neighbor. Now he was the representative of a being of unimaginable power; but still, Ronnie thought, *This man is speaking the truth*.

"What do you mean when you say that you love us?" Lorraine asked.

Used-to-be-Claude turned to the angry, shy, frightened, and very, very brave young woman and said, "I am as any other being. When I saw you struggle for your life, it made me understand what might have been, can never be. And when Friend Ronnie made the choice, in an instant, to save your life rather than let you go, I saw him through eyes that so respected you. This double knowledge increased my feeling all the more."

"But you told Ronnie that we were just bugs to you," she said, losing her anger and her fear for a moment.

"It is true," Used-to-be-Claude said with a sad smile on his lips. "But I am also at one with all beings. And even omnipotence can feel unique love. I love you two every bit as much as I loathe Inglo."

"But you just met us," Lorraine reasoned.

"And I have known the Laz for billions of your years. Shouldn't I understand them by now? Instead I nurse my hatred of them."

"But if that's true, why don't you just go out there and get Ma Lin?" Lorraine asked, her voice now strong and clear. "You're the one with all the power. Why don't you just wave your hand and pull him back behind that door?"

"Because Inglo and I are so deeply intertwined that we cannot see each other in the world at large. He is me and therefore forever concealed from my senses."

"That's why we could see him," Ronnie offered to Lorraine, "but Used-to-be-Claude here cain't."

The off-white girl was, once again, working into a rage at the Deity and her murderer. She was, in her heart, destroying them both. This talking was too much, and she wanted it to end now.

"That is how I felt, Friend Lorraine!" the great voice boomed around them.

Ronnie glanced at Used-to-be-Claude. He was standing stock-still, his hands frozen in the gesture of a shrug.

"That is how I felt," the great voice declared again, "when I realized I had been created to torture, kill, and maim. I wanted it to stop, but first I had to free myself and throw all my power into resistance."

Both Ronnie and Lorraine stood up straight, electrified by the communication that entered through every sense and nerve. They could hear, imagine, taste, and feel the pain that the Silver Box had known.

Lorraine began to cry.

Ronnie was trembling from both fear and rage.

"Go now," the disembodied Silver Box ordered.

The body of Claude Festerling got to its feet, moving like a puppet on intelligently deft strings. The corpse raised its left arm and pointed with a long elegant finger at the black and glittery wall. The material fell away, creating a portal that opened onto a dirt path inside a stone cave.

"You need to know some things, learn some shit, and find the tools you'll help you," Used-to-be-Claude said in his most human voice. "You need to take this journey that will lead you back to where you began."

With these words said, the corpse fell lifeless to the floor and the two human representatives of technological divinity went through the doorway like Adam and Eve, of their own accord, fleeing Eden.

TWELVE

LORRAINE FELL AND Ronnie Bottoms, two already greatly changed human beings, found themselves on a rock and dirt path, maybe twelve feet wide, that ran at a slight incline through a tunnel that might have also been a cave.

There was a dim luminescence coming from far up ahead, allowing them to see however poorly on the underground rocky road.

"This is better, right?" Ronnie said.

"What is?"

"Just dirt and rocks and stuff. I was goin' kinda nuts with all that crazy shit. What you think? We in a cave somewhere in Central Park?"

"I never heard of any caves like this in the park," Lorraine said.

"But maybe the Silver Box made it for us to walk toward where we goin' at. You know, to get ready for what we got to do."

"And just what are we going to do?"

"You know . . . grab that Vietnamese dude, that Ma Lin, and drag him back to the boulders where him and old SB could have it out."

"And do you believe what he's telling us?"

"SB?"

"Whatever."

As he was walking a step behind, Ronnie reached out to touch his fellow travcler's elbow. She flinched away from him, pressing her back up against the rocky wall. She didn't look frightened. Spite curled her lip, and something like anger tightened her multicolored eyes.

"Don't put your hands on me," she said.

Ronnie put up his hands in a gesture of surrender and said. "Look, there ain't no way around what I done to you. I tried to rape you. I definitely killed you. And if you snuck up behind me in this cave and cracked me in the head with a rock, I couldn't blame ya. I did what I did and it was wrong. And the onliest reason I come back to save you was because you threatened to turn me in. There ain't no gettin' around that. There ain't no forgiveness for that.

"But you know what you did and you know that I took the blood and fat and bone outta my own body and brought you all the way back to where you was. Not like Claude Whatever but alive again.

"And so if SB wanna tell me that he's buildin' a bodega in the middle'a the sun, I won't say it's impossible. If he say that he's gonna kill all the people in all the world, I'm inclined to believe him and to try and do what he says.

"I mean I wouldn't mind bein' Adam an' Eve and all, but that's not you and me, not by a long shot."

Lorraine fought back the rage she was feeling. The killer's words had purchase in her breast. She didn't want to understand him, but there was a bond there somewhere. She didn't need the Hegelian dialectic to know that her path was set out in front of her like the one-way path of that underground tunnel.

"You think the light up ahead is the park?" she said instead of what she was thinking.

"I ain't got no idea," Ronnie said, flashing a rare smile. "But I do know that that's the only way we got to go."

"I guess some things are pretty simple," Lorraine said.

"Yes, ma'am," Ronnie said, dredging up the manners his mother tried to teach him when he was young and half wild.

ALMOST AN HOUR later Ronnie and Lorraine climbed out of the cave mouth into a beautiful sunlit day in a forest that was deep and green, and seemed to go on forever.

"Where are we?" Ronnie asked for both of them.

"This is the road the Silver Box put us on," Lorraine replied.

Ronnie nodded and they both walked on the path that led out from the cave and through the great cedar and pine and redwood forest.

The packed dirt of this path was yellow, and the road was much wider, at least a hundred feet across.

They walked for another hour or so without speaking. The sun seemed to shine not only on their heads and shoulders but also through them. The air was crisp and cool but they were warm because they were moving at a good clip.

"*THERE'S A STREAM* over there," Lorraine said, ending their long silence. "Are you thirsty?"

Down by the flowing water, they found ground berries that were somewhat like strawberries but hardier and with a tougher skin. They ate their fill and drank deeply. After that they leaned against a convenient boulder, allowing the setting sun to shine on them.

Ronnie lifted his right hand and studied it. "You think that there's really millions of bugs crawlin' on our skin?" he asked.

"I was your victim," Lorraine said.

"What?"

"That Silver Box said that we both had been guilty, but I didn't do anything to you. I was going to school, jogging in the park. . . . I wanted to help people. I wanted to understand how the world works."

Ronnie nodded, not looking at his fellow traveler.

"Say something," Lorraine commanded.

Ronnie turned toward the woman who had poured out of his body and formed on the ground in front of him, the woman he breathed life into. This miracle was something that only a god could perform, but he didn't feel like God.

"I was up in Attica for two years on a nickel sentence," he said after a long pause.

"Yes," she said, "you're the criminal."

"That's true but it ain't what I'm sayin'. Of all the bad things that can happen to you in the joint, the worst is how borin' it always is. You cain't go nowhere and there ain't nuthin' to do."

"What do you expect?" Lorraine asked. "You committed a crime."

"I know," Ronnie acceded. "I know. And I had done twelve things wrong for the one they got me for. What I'm tryin' to say is that there ain't nuthin' to do in prison but eat, shit, fuck, fight, and talk. And mostly we talked. A lot we talked about shittin', eatin', fightin', and fuckin,' but there was other things too.

"We was all guilty and we knew it too. Some was proud. But even if you wasn't proud, you had to ack like it to keep people from thinkin' you was a bitch. And if you have to be proud, or ack like you proud, then you talk differently about the people you might'a hurt. You start to believe that just because somebody was your victim and you're guilty, that still don't make them innocent."

"I didn't attack myself," Lorraine claimed.

"No. No, you didn't. But you run down the street past poor, sick, uneducated, homeless, and hopeless people with yo' fine ass and your pockets full'a money. I belonged in prison but that don't make you innocent. I think that's what SB was sayin'. It's easy to find guilt all up and down the streets. But how's all that no-good shit gonna be there, and here you are so innocent that you don't have nuthin' to do with it?"

This thought wasn't alien to Lorraine. She had studied original sin and the various interpretations of social and socialist revolutions. She had written a term paper on the paradox of capital punishment. And, sitting there with her own killer, she realized that all of this had been in her head, that she'd never had to answer for the crimes of her culture and her class; nor did she truly believe that she should be held responsible.

This feeling of innocence somehow caused her shame. This shame made her angry and the anger brought out the unfamiliar feeling of belligerence.

"I don't care," she said. "I'm not like you."

"No, honey, you not. But here we are on the same road, and you the one brought me here—ain't no question about that."

THIRTEEN

THE TWO SAT for a long time after devouring dozens of berries and many drafts of sweet-tasting water. When the sun began to go down they decided to rest until morning.

The twilight in the uncharted high forest was beautiful but when the sun set and the moon rose over a far mountain, the air turned cold. Lorraine began to shiver. Ronnie put his arm around her and pulled her close.

"Get off me," Lorraine complained. "I don't need you."

"I know you don't, girl," the killer said. "Maybe you ain't cold, but I'm freezin'. I just wanted to get a little warm, that's all."

"That's all?"

"Come on, baby, you need me to tell you again how my dick ain't workin' right?"

"Do you have to use that language?"

"It's the only language I got."

Lorraine turned her back to Ronnie and pressed into his embrace. When they came together, they were enveloped in warmth that was both physical and somehow emotional. Ronnie giggled, maybe for the first time since before adolescence, and Lorraine smiled, forgetting about the philosophies of if and why; about the crimes against her or ideas she believed but did not accept.

Swathed in warmth neither one had known since infancy they fell into a sleep so profound that the world around them seemed to fall away.

As they slept they didn't notice the chromium skinned antlike insects that swarmed around Lorraine's eyes, biting her over and over with preordained precision and accuracy.

IN THE MORNING Ronnie rose first. He went across the stream and into the forest to relieve himself. He was just zipping up the brown pants he'd bought in the thrift shop when Lorraine screamed.

Running back to their bed of grasses and soil, he saw the young woman standing upright, moving from side to side, and holding her face with both hands.

"What's wrong?" Ronnie shouted, running to her side.

"I'm blind! I'm blind!"

"Let me see," Ronnie said. "What's wrong?"

He grabbed her wrists, pulling at them to get a look at her face—but when he tugged, her head moved with her hands.

"I got to look at it if I'm gonna do anything," he reasoned.

Lorraine fell to her knees and Ronnie descended with her. She continued resisting him and he had to consciously keep himself from forcing her to expose her face.

Finally he let her go and said, "Please, Lorraine, I just wanna help."

Slowly, hesitantly Lorraine lowered her hands. Her eyelids and the flesh from the middle of her forehead down to the bridge of her nose were red and very swollen, effectively shutting her eyes.

"What is it?" she cried. "I can't see."

"It looks like bug bites."

"Bugs? Why would the Silver Box go out of his way to make a place so completely and then leave bugs to hurt somebody like this?"

Ronnie wondered too but he didn't echo his companion. Instead he took her hands in his. "It's just bug bites," he said. "They're swollen but they'll go down. We should get some cold water on'em and I bet the swellin'll go down soon."

"You think so?"

"I do."

"How long could that take?"

"When I get a mosquito bite, it usually lasts a day, two at most."

"Two days," she wailed.

"It's okay, Lorraine. I'm right here wit' you, girl. I promise you that."

He took her down to the stream and, using cupped hands, poured water over her eyes.

"That feels really good," she said.

"Don't it sting?"

"No, the water makes it feel relaxed. I think you're right about it helping."

"You think maybe we should wait here until you could

see again?" Ronnie asked as he went about plucking the deep red ground berries.

"No," she said. "Silver Box didn't give us a deadline but he made it sound like we had to act fast. We have to keep moving."

"But he said that time stopped until we get back."

"Maybe he meant it stopped until when we got here," she argued. "We can't take the chance."

"Okay. You just put your arm in mine and I'll tell ya if there's a rock or tree branch in the way."

Lorraine smiled and reached out for her killer's crooked arm. They got to their feet and continued on the unlikely path of their lives.

As THE DAY progressed they made good time, feeling energized by the sun and air, the ground berries and also somehow by their closeness.

Ronnie noticed that a new kind of tree was appearing here and there. This new vegetation had dark bark on thick trunks with huge outcropping branches that bore light green leaves the size and shape of one-man kayaks. The wary side of Ronnie's streetwise mind wondered what this new kind of tree might mean for them.

"There's a little light getting in between my eyelids," Lorraine said before he could mention the trees to her.

"That's good," he said. "That means you're gettin' better."

They walked arm in arm, as close as lovers or siblings or small children using the buddy system on a school outing.

"Even though I was mad at you, I still wanted to jump your bones again last night," she said after a while.

"I never had a woman do that to me before."

"Did you like it?"

"It was wild. You know like if you was a man."

"I thought you said you did that in prison."

"Yeah, but I was always the one on top. You know I never let a woman do too much with sex. I guess I never even wondered about what she felt."

"What do you think now?"

"That I never knew nuthin' before we met."

"Maybe you'll regret it by the time this is over."

"I don't think so."

"Why not?"

"Because of my great-uncle Phil Goldstone, my mother's mother's brother."

"What about him?"

"He was in the war that Ma Lin fought in."

"Vietnam?"

"There's a rock in front'a your left foot."

They stopped and Lorraine nudged her left foot out until her shod toe tapped the four-inch-high obstruction. Stepping over the rock, they went on.

"Uncle Phil hated everything about the war," Ronnie continued. "He said that he hated the enemy and he hated the white government for sendin' him there. But he made his best friends and had the greatest times of his life there. He hated it, but he loved it more'n anything too."

"And that's how you feel about me?" She hugged his arm closer.

"That's how I feel about everything. My whole life's been a war, and you the last fight in that war. I won the fight but then I lost it too. And now . . . now I'm free and I don't regret a thing. I cain't."

"Why not?"

"Because it brought me here."

Three steps of silence and suddenly Lorraine pulled away and started scratching furiously at her sides and all around the waist. She made panting sounds and was in such distress that she fell to the ground scratching, scratching. Ronnie got down with her, putting his hands up her dress to help.

"Don't do that!"

"I have to, Lorraine. I got to see what's wrong."

Lorraine stopped struggling and lay stiff on the ground. Ronnie lifted the blue fabric. . . . Bug bites covered her abdomen and sides going down under the line of her panties, coming out at her thighs, and traveling down another five or six inches.

"The bugs must be in your clothes," he said. "I'll carry you back to that pond we saw and we could wash'em there."

Lorraine yowled loudly and Ronnie hoped that insects were the largest creatures in that wood.

HE WALKED HER out into the middle of the deep pond. It was about thirty-five feet across, fed by the stream that they had lain next to the night before and three or four other rivulets.

When the girl was shoulder high in the natural pool, he

had her take off her clothes. These he took to the shore and rinsed over and over, finally beating them with rocks.

"Ronnie, are you there?" Lorraine called from her semi-darkness.

"Right here beatin' on these clothes. You know if there was any bugs left, they all dead and crushed. How you doin'?"

"The water soothes the itch. It's cold but I like it."

"It's really pretty here. When your swelling goes down, you're gonna love it."

"You know what's so crazy, Ronnie?"

"What's that, Lore?"

"That we just accept all this as real. I mean, it's impossible, right?"

"It always felt like that for me," the once brooding and ravenous brute said.

"Like what?"

"Like nuthin's real but I couldn't stop it anyway. Locked doors, hunger, me hatin' myself for the things I never did and the things I never did right."

Lorraine turned her blind gaze toward her companion. There was a question in her mind that went unspoken.

"You surprised that a niggah like me think about things too?"

"I guess I am," she said. "I mean, I don't think that name about you but what you just said, that question and that feeling has been in my heart for as far back as I could remember."

"It's like when somebody you know die, right?" Ronnie added. "You feel like they should be alive, like they must be somewhere. All you got to do is figure out the right way to turn or somethin' special you could say."

"But if you did, it would turn out like Claude Festerling," Lorraine added. "And me too if you hadn't come back."

Lorraine pushed herself toward the sound of Ronnie Bottoms's voice and came out of the water only a few feet away. He wrung her clothes with all his strength and then reached out.

"You'll be cool in these."

"Thank you, Mr. Bottoms."

FOURTEEN

THAT NIGHT THEY slept on the flat top of a boulder far away from any water, reasoning that whatever had bitten Lorraine was an insect living in or near the stream. Ronnie stayed awake for a long time after she was asleep to make sure no biting bugs crawled up or flew down.

He finally fell asleep and did not see the approach of the huge form of a woolly beast that was at least forty feet in height and twice that in length. The nearly silent four-legged creature moved through the woods like shadow. From its shaggy, egg-shaped head, a long and needle-thin bone slowly stretched out until it reached the sleeping young man, pricking him on every joint and at the back of his neck.

The slight discomfort from the venom of the mammal's sting caused Ronnie to twist and turn until he came to rest on his back with legs straight and arms down at his sides.

Its work done, the needle withdrew and the shadow beast backed away, merging with the moonlit shadows of the nighttime forest.

"Ronnie, I'm cold," Lorraine complained in her sleep.

He imagined turning on his side and holding the young coed. In his dream he did this but not within the reality of the Silver Box.

LORRAINE WOKE UP with the sun in her eyes. The itching was gone, and not only could she see again but the world looked clearer than it ever had. She jumped to her feet with unaccustomed ease and looked down on her companion.

Lowering herself again to her knees, and seeing that his eyes were open, she said, "Wake up, sleepyhead."

"I'm awake," he said, "just not up."

"Then come on. I can see and all the bites are gone."

"That's great," Ronnie said. "You know I'd get up wit' ya but my arms and legs are stiff as sticks. I cain't even turn my head."

"Why not?"

"Just another trick SB be pullin', I suppose."

"You can't move at all?"

"Been gettin' stiffer and stiffer every minute. It's hard for me even to open my mouf. It hurts where that cop broke the bone and I don't even think I'll be able to talk after while."

"Don't be scared," Lorraine said. "I'm here."

"I know you are" were the last words he spoke for some time.

————

LORRAINE SAT BESIDE the paralyzed young man for the next few hours—talking.

"I'm sorry for getting so mad," she said at one point. "I mean, not sorry but I'm just saying that I understand what it is that drove you. And even though you didn't want to save me, you did anyway. Only you could have done it. But I don't know why . . . I mean, you know, I'm really mad. You did a terrible thing to me and I hate you for it partly but . . . I never got anything but A's in school, you know. I was always the best student in every class and I thought that meant that . . . that . . ."

Ronnie listened and appreciated that she sat there next to him, keeping him safe from whatever might attack a paralyzed man in the deep woods. Any kind of animal or bird could start eating him out there and he wouldn't have been able even to try and shoo it away.

Ronnie had no sensation except for a thrumming that started in his chest and traveled through his arms and legs, down along his fingers and toes. The vibrations passed through his bones and reminded him, as so many things did, of his mother's wordless songs when he was little.

". . . I could see in the way the police treated you, and in the things my father had to say, why black people have it so hard," Lorraine was saying. He noticed that she was talking faster and faster. "I mean, you were still wrong to do that to me and if it wasn't for how it happened, I'd—I might really have hit you in the head with a rock."

Her voice carried sharp anger. She could have hit him now. Worse . . . she could just leave him to be eaten by birds and foxes. There were foxes in the eastern forests; he'd learned that in third grade.

Third grade was a good year, Ronnie thought. Miss Peters was a very kindly woman who would make him stay behind in her classroom at recess and over the lunch break to keep him occupied and off the playground, where he was likely to get into fights. She talked to him about foxes and forests and why the smartest people in the world knew that they didn't know anything for sure.

"Ronnie?" Lorraine said.

He tried to turn his eyes to show that he'd heard, but he couldn't even do that.

"My legs are all jittery," the girl said. "I'm going to take a run up the path a little ways. It'll only be a few minutes. I'll be right back."

IN THE PERIPHERY of sight, he saw Lorraine jump off the fifteen-foot-high boulder. He worried that she might have broken her neck on landing until he heard her call, "I'll be back soon."

He wondered if she had abandoned him; if she had decided to go on because the world was about to be destroyed and her parents might die. He would have left her. At least the old him would have.

A moment of darkness filled the world, and Ronnie realized he was still blinking. Whatever had paralyzed his movements left his heart beating and allowed his lids to work on his eyes.

The thrumming in his bones somehow kept him from being frightened. It was his mother, and the feeling of life so pure and so strong that the thing Ronnie wanted most to do was laugh. And even that, the feeling of a laugh that wouldn't come out, made the young brawler glad.

He'd never killed anybody before Lorraine, and somehow God—even if God was a machine and not an old white man in a white beard—had turned the clock back a little bit and given him a chance to undo what had been done. The forest was beautiful and the white girl had taken off all her clothes in front of him and nobody got hurt.

It was at that moment Ronnie accepted his death. Maybe, he thought, he had died in the police interrogation room or in that Rikers cell when his back was turned and somebody came up on him with a toothbrush turned into a knife. Maybe he had died and come to this imaginary place to have his last thoughts like prayers asking for forgiveness for what he'd done wrong. He had tried in this dream to save the white girl. He had said he was sorry even though people always told him sorry was not enough.

But sorry was all Ronnie had. He tried in his mind to make things right. He dreamed the girl back to life and imagined the great Silver Box that had God inside. He said he would do what's right and if that wasn't enough, if that didn't make things okay, he'd have to go along with it because there was nothing else to do.

When Ronnie blinked, he imagined the world coming to an end, but instead a large, emerald green bird flew up and landed on his chest. The long-taloned bird had bloodred eyes. It turned its head from side to side, examining Ronnie.

Maybe this, the ex-con thought, was his personal executioner studying him for the deathblow.

FIFTEEN

LORRAINE RAN DOWN the wide yellow path with long loping strides. She had no way of gauging her speed but she was going somewhere between twenty-five and thirty miles an hour, faster than any human being and with more stamina than almost any creature in the history of creatures. Every now and then she'd bound six or seven feet into the air, landing as lightly as a butterfly on a rose blossom.

The faster she went, the more she laughed. It was the bug bites, she knew, that had transformed her. Bug bites caused by the Silver Box to give her the speed and agility and the ability to run like this. This was her opportunity to be the woman she had always dreamed of being; with a clear eye and sure feet—the offspring of a goddess tired of men having everything.

LORRAINE RAN AND ran, thinking about her body and not the philosophies of Hannah Arendt and Karl Marx.

She was a part of the packed yellow-dirt road and the deep blue sky. There was no such thing as time or necessity, just running faster and faster on a single breath.

After a while, she had no idea how long, she veered off the path and into the woods, moving deftly between and over braches and roots that rose up out of the ground like tentacles from the sea in some nineteenth-century Jules Verne novel.

With ease and unaccustomed poise, she climbed the thick-bodied, dark-bark tree in front of her; ran up into the widely spaced branches, among the huge tapered leaves. At the topmost branch, she had to stop but in her heart she wanted to run on the thin air up to the clouds. This desire was so powerful that she cried out and jumped, only to fall back on the upper branch.

She could hear her steady breathing in the silent canopy of the woods. There her mind slowed down. She realized that her speed had somehow suspended her intellectual predilections. This she took as a blessing. There had never been a moment in her memory where her mind gave up control to her body.

Her long steady breaths were like the wind through an echo chamber. She saw the world around her as it was: composed of material things, not as metaphors or portents, not as false reality but just events she would never fully understand. One of those events was the ten- and eleven-foot-long seedpods that grew under the huge leaves of the unfamiliar tree.

———

THE GREEN BIRD'S red eyes were bright beads like the scarlet danger lights on the dashboard of a car. It stared at the hapless young man and then pecked at his cheek. After this tentative attack the bird skipped back a step, afraid Ronnie might grab at it. But when no retaliation was forthcoming, it returned to its perch on his chest and pecked at the skin just above Ronnie's left eye.

Ronnie understood then that he would be killed slowly and methodically by this rooster-sized predator. Maybe this was his judgment; maybe this was hell, and for the rest of time, the green demon bird would eat off his face and eyes over and over again.

The green bird cocked its head to reconnoiter Ronnie's features.

"Hola, hey! Get out of here!" came the bullet-fast words of Lorraine's voice.

The bird startled backwards, did an avian double take, and then fluttered away. The next thing that came into Ronnie's field of vision was Lorraine's olive-toned gaunt face with its brown and blue eyes. She was smiling down on him.

"Your new friend looked hungry," she said.

She rubbed his left brow with her right hand and when she pulled the hand away, there was blood on the thumb pad.

"He played rough," she said.

In his mind Ronnie grinned.

Lorraine hopped up to her feet and hefted a huge brown canoe over her head. Her grin was magnificent and victorious. "It's half of a seedpod from this fat tree with leaves as big as bedsheets," she said. She rapped the side of the long and mostly straight piece of vegetation making the sound of a door being knocked upon. "It's really hard. I'm gonna put it down on the rock right below you and roll you in. Then I'll drag you and it down to the yellow road. Once I build up some speed, I think I can slide you along after me with no problem."

Lorraine moved out of sight for a few moments and then appeared again with a hard and fast grin plastered on her face.

"Okay," she said. "I'm going to roll you over now. If you don't want me to, then just shake your head. . . ."

Lorraine laughed and then pushed against Ronnie's left side. He didn't budge but she kept laughing. She moved out of range and then she was there again, ramming into him. He rolled once, twice, and then was in free fall until he came to a jolting stop inside the pod.

It was a tight fit and he was on his side looking at the silvery, hairlike fur that was there to cushion the seeds before they scattered out to become trees.

"That was a good shot, huh?" Lorraine said.

She pulled and pushed against his inert body until he was mostly on his back in the coffinlike space.

"The hardest thing was," Lorraine said, "finding one of these pods with a curved stem that I could get around my shoulder. Watch out, it's going to be bumpy on the way down."

Ronnie felt the pod being raised from somewhere up beyond his head. For a few seconds he was bouncing back and forth inasmuch as the confined space allowed and then he came to a halt—momentarily.

The sky overhead was cloudless and the sun was nowhere

in sight, but its radiance was evident in the leaves of the trees that surrounded him. The pod wavered this way and that, and then it was moving, making the hissing sound of a sled being dragged through snow.

At first they went at a sluggish pace, slower than a normal walk. But slowly they picked up speed until Ronnie felt that he was in a gypsy cab in the early morning after a night of partying up in Harlem.

Snug in the giant seedpod, moving as fast as an automobile under an azure sky, with the swishing sound of the pod against the ground blocking out all other sound—Ronnie felt a contradictory sense of freedom. As long as he could remember, he'd been struggling against something: his siblings, the foster care authority, the police . . . He'd been stalking the streets, likely to fight with anyone he came in contact with. He'd been shot, stabbed, beaten, incarcerated, chained, abandoned, and even raped; this last humiliation he could not admit to his new friend. Every one of those experiences, and dozens of others, were like the door behind which the evil alien race, the Laz, was kept by Used-to-be-Claude. He had walked through each door that contained his suffering. But now under this impossible sky, he couldn't even lift a finger to get himself into trouble.

This day was a new day for the first time that Ronnie could remember. He didn't mind his paralysis. There was nowhere he needed to go.

HOURS LATER, WHEN Ronnie wasn't even paying attention to the tops of trees and depth of blue, he became aware of pain. It was the spot over his left eye where the demon bird had pecked him, where the carnivorous bird took his second beakful of human flesh at the beginning of a feast that might have lasted for days if not for Loraine.

The pain grew, traveling down his face into his neck and spine. From there it followed the thrumming into his joints. Ronnie could perceive his entire skeleton like a series of burning stars that made him a constellation, the kind Miss Peters had taught him about in the third grade.

The Dead Man, Ronnie thought, that would be the name of his constellation: a floating corpse thrown out from its coffin by earthquake or flood and then lifted to the heavens by God.

His joints were like fiery sparklers that children ran around with on the Fourth of July. His being was on fire but still he couldn't speak a word.

At one point, he saw off in the woods behind them an impossibly huge animal. It had shaggy brown hair like a Rasta, an egg-shaped head, and big sorrowful eyes looking down on him.

Ronnie tried to call out, to tell Lorraine about the spectacle and the danger, but he couldn't move a muscle, and the vision soon faded into the distance.

WHEN THE SKY began darkening, the pod slowed gradually until coming to a halt. Lorraine appeared there above him again. This time her face was streaked with sweat.

"That was great," she said. "I never felt so good in my

life. I bet we went over a hundred miles and I didn't hardly feel it until we stopped."

Ronnie didn't mind the pain. He was glad to have a friend.

"We're next to another pond," she said. "I'll bring you some water. I hope you can drink some."

Lorraine disappeared for a time and then came back with her cupped hands lined with leaves and brimming with water. She tried to pour the liquid into his mouth but there was no give there. Somehow, though, the water seemed to cause the thrumming and burning sensations to merge.

Ronnie wanted to crawl out of his skin. He felt like the snakes that Miss Peters had spoken of so often; the creature that shed its skin and emerged bigger and stronger than ever.

SIXTEEN

FOR HOURS, FROM early evening into night, Lorraine sat next to the seedpod sled, regaling Ronnie with bland stories about her family life: summer camps and chess club, her first kiss and how her father used to carry her on his shoulders.

"One time my mom took me to Saunders and Son to buy a dress for a birthday party I was supposed to go to," she said under a sliver moon. "I was five and the birthday girl was Janet Powers. She used to make fun of me because I had a lisp, and so I didn't want to go. My mom just thought that all little kids were friends and accepted the invitation for me without asking. But when I told her that I didn't want a dress because I didn't want to go, and why, she bought me a pair of red cowboy boots and we went to the botanical gardens in Brooklyn instead."

Her voice was normal again but she went on and on. To anyone else the stories might have been dreary, but Ronnie hadn't had much of a childhood and he imagined himself

with her life, wearing those red cowboy boots and running around all kinds of flowers.

At some point she stopped talking, either that or Ronnie
just fell asleep.

IN THE MORNING Ronnie raised his hand to the scab on
his brow without thinking. Next he grabbed the edges of
the pod and hefted himself up into a seated position. It
was then that he remembered being paralyzed for an entire
day.

Experimenting with his restored mobility, he climbed out
of the pod.

He was standing there on the side of the yellow dirt road,
and Lorraine was walking toward him, her hands cupped
again.

She dropped the water and shouted. "Ronnie!"

"Hey."

She ran to him and put her hands on his shoulders. "You
grew," she said.

Looking down on her, he saw what she meant: He was
taller and there was more girth to his form. He wasn't
heavy, as before Lorraine's rebirth, but much stronger
looking.

"How did you do that?" she asked.

"I ain't done nuthin' in the last twenty-four," he replied.
"It's just this crazy place. I mean, how could you run so fast
and carry me like that? You was goin' fast as a car on the
highway."

"I had to," she said. "It felt like I had to keep on moving

faster and faster until all the thoughts were completely gone from my head."

"Well, how'm I gonna keep up wit' you now? I bet I won't be able to move like that."

"It's okay," she said, exhibiting a brilliant smile. "I got it all out carrying you along. I could run if I have to, but it's not eating at me anymore."

THEY ATE RAW fish from a large lake and more of the dark red ground berries. After that they walked in the bright sun of the deep forest.

"Where do you think we are?" Lorraine asked at one point.

"Like a hospital," Ronnie replied.

"A hospital?"

"Yeah. First you got your medicine and went blind and then got fast. I was all locked up like in the prison ward but they didn't need bars and restraints. I think Used-to-be-Claude is gettin' us ready to go up against Ma Lin."

"Wow!" Lorraine exclaimed. "Wouldn't that be great? If a clinic would be a forest full of bugs and animals and medicine waters? Wow."

Her last word seemed to grow and grow until it was a roar.

Standing in the road before them was a large creature; imposing like a bear but also lithe and long like an alley cat. It was covered with midnight dark bristling fur and had bright, hateful eyes. Ronnie figured that the beast was at least one and a half times his size and weight before the

Silver Box and Lorraine changed him. Its brilliant orange eyes were filled with bad intentions.

Lorraine screamed and turned to run. Her quick movement caught the attention of the bearcat. It took off after her. The animal was so fast that it might have caught her but Ronnie jumped and wrapped his arms around its middle. He threw the creature down on the dirt road and then grabbed it by its pelt along the spine and hefted the thing high above his head. It writhed in this impossible hold, but before it could get free, Ronnie threw it with all his might. The black bearcat bounced on the road fifteen feet away and then landed another five feet along. Instantly it was on its feet staring at the young black man.

"Come on, mothahfuckah, try it," Ronnie said between clenched teeth.

Whether the predator understood the words or just the tone, it hesitated and then ran off into the woods.

"That was amazing," Lorraine said. She was standing behind him with a clublike tree branch in her hands. "That thing must've weighed at least four hundred pounds."

"It smelled bad too."

Lorraine giggled, dropped her club, and kissed her companion on the cheek.

Ronnie had seen friends kiss like this before in churches and on street corners when there was a chance meeting. It wasn't usually sexual but just a kind of hello. With the solitary exception of his mother, he had never kissed or been kissed in this manner. Touching the spot where her lips had butted up against his face, Ronnie forgot about the deadly bearcat.

"What?" Lorraine asked.

"Um," he uttered.

"Did I do something wrong?"

"No, girl. I was just thinkin' 'bout how fast you are and how I got so much stronger. Used-to-be-Claude must be really worried about this Laz thing."

"You just picked up that thing and threw it."

"And the world looks different," he added.

"The way I see things is weird too," Lorraine said, "but I can't say how."

"Neither me."

"You think this all has to do with Ma Lin?"

Ronnie allowed the question to move around in his mind a moment. Before he could reformulate his belief, a humming seemed to rise up out of the ground at his feet and he was forced to close his eyes against the mounting barrier of sound.

When the noise subsided he opened his eyes again and found himself, once more, on his knees facing a similarly positioned Lorraine. They were in the nest of boulders again; the place where Ronnie had killed and then resurrected his new friend.

"Did we ever go anywhere?" Ronnie asked.

"Yes, we did," Lorraine said. "I think that we were in the stars like huge nebular clouds. I think that the Silver Box is everywhere and we were there with him. We were in a clinic just like you said and now we're ready to go after Ma Lin. The Silver Box is making us go to war."

"I don't think so," Ronnie said with certainty. "It's up to us if we want to save the Earth or make it all over again."

"It's so crazy to believe that two little people like us could have such responsibility."

"But it's not just you and me," Ronnie said, wondering as he spoke where the words were coming from. "It's you and me and the Silver Box and that dead thing that wasn't dead inside. It's me killin' you and you makin' me bring you back and us bein' watched when there was something else tryin' to get away."

"So we go after Ma Lin?"

"Yeah."

"What do we do when we find him?"

"We got to find him first," Ronnie said. He rose to his feet and put out a hand to Lorraine.

"You told him to go to the zoo," she said, and then she laughed.

Looking at Ronnie, Lorraine wondered if the young woman she had been really died and was replaced with someone else who only thought she was that girl.

SEVENTEEN

THERE WERE POLICEMEN and park officials coming in
and out of the zoo entrance. Access was barred to the public,
and dozens of people were standing outside. Among the
crowd were a few television crews with reporters talking to
the cameras.

One apple butter brown young woman was having a
conversation with a cameraman's lens.

"That's right, Jack," she answered into the camera, "a
man somehow got into the lion's cage and killed two of
the cats. No one saw a weapon, but zoo officials say that
both a knife and some kind of bludgeon were used." There
was a pause where the woman looked as if she was listening, and then she said, "Yes, it really is amazing. Usually
when a person climbs into the wild animal cages, they're the
ones in danger. But the lions are definitely dead and the man
who killed them disappeared into the underground cata-
combs where there are confinement areas for the animals.

Police have blocked all the exits and assure us that they will have him in custody soon. . . ."

"YOU THINK WE should try to get in there and go after him?" Lorraine asked. Her legs were getting jittery again. Alternately she was pumping both heels almost as if she were running in place.

"Uh-uh," Ronnie grunted. "Too many people around here. They'd just get in the way. He's down there lookin' for the Silver Box. When he don't find it, he'll come out on his own."

"But we're supposed to bring him back."

"That's what we're after," Ronnie agreed, "but Ma Lin's after somethin' too."

"The Silver Box," Lorraine said.

"But," Ronnie added, "the Box and the Laz thing cain't see each other, so the onliest thing Ma Lin could come aftah is us. All we got to do is get somewhere where we're alone, and he'll be tryin' to get us."

"Like he did with those lions?"

"Just like that."

"If two lions couldn't hurt him, what could we do?"

"You scared?" Ronnie asked.

Lorraine considered the question honestly, as a child might. She wondered about the lions and fear and suddenly, brilliantly smiled.

"Not at all," she said. "I'm faster than any lion and you're probably stronger than one."

THEY WENT TO a fairly isolated part of the park not far from the place where the Silver Box resided. After climbing up into the boughs of a century oak, they perched next to each other in the branches—waiting.

"It's kinda strange when we're next to each other, isn't it?" Lorraine asked.

"Yeah. It feels like the way I did when I was a kid and my mama would hold me."

"When I close my eyes," Lorraine said, straining for the right words, "it's like I'm floating in space and there's a drummer playing just for me."

"I guess you'n me is like brother and sister, huh, Lore."

"That's what my father calls me—Lore. How did you know?"

"We got the same blood," he said. "I mean, probably everybody and everything in the world gots the same blood, but somehow you'n me can feel it, 'specially when we're next to each other."

Ronnie saw the words' impact on Lorraine, and then her blue eye flashed as if a light was shone upon it.

"Something's wrong," she said.

"I don't mean to hurt anybody!" a man yelled.

Turning his gaze upward, Ronnie saw a man's form hurtling down toward them. Images and thoughts scurried through the young man's mind: First he realized that he wouldn't be able to get out of the way and that he probably wouldn't be able to ward off any blow; second he recognized the man as Ma Lin; and third he saw that there was something odd about the attacker's hands.

"I'm sorry!" Ma Lin was screaming when Lorraine, as a blur, jumped at him, colliding with his midsection.

When Ronnie saw that his newfound soul mate and mortal foe were tumbling down out of the tree toward the ground, he jumped after them.

Lorraine and Ma Lin hit the ground first but they sprawled where Ronnie landed on his feet.

"I can't help myself!" Ma Lin shouted. "I don't want to!"

His actions, however, didn't match his complaints.

Neither of his arms ended in hands. His left wrist sported what looked like a bayonet made from hardened, olive-colored flesh and his right was a fist turned solid without fingers or thumb.

Ma Lin jabbed at Ronnie with the blade-hand but the young man sidestepped the thrust and hit his attacker with a solid left hook. Ma Lin fell into a cartwheel movement that brought him to a standing position five feet away. The ex–military policeman lunged once again at Ronnie, this time with both arms raised for attack.

"I can't help myself!" he yelled, moving almost as fast as Lorraine.

Before Ma Lin reached Ronnie, there was a loud knock and then he was on the ground and Lorraine was standing there with yet another branch-club in her hands.

Immediately Ma Lin was up and jumping toward the girl.

Ronnie leaped and struck with both hands balled into a single fist. Ma Lin grunted and went down hard but he bounced up again, deftly using the blade hand to pierce Ronnie's chest.

"I'm sorry!" Ma Lin screamed. "I'm so sorry!"

Ronnie fell backwards, feeling the blade unsheathe itself from his breast. His heart pumped once and the range of light diminished by half. Blood flowed copiously from the gash in his chest. There was a woman's scream and a loud cracking sound. Ronnie's heart pumped again and the light diminished again by half. Another scream, crack, beat, and Ronnie saw the ground coming up toward his face. He knew he must be falling but this did not change the impression of the ground moving up toward him. He smiled, heard a scream and crack, expected the ground to hit him, but his face and the turf did not meet. He blinked then and wondered if that was the last time his eyes would close. His heart pumped and all his skin felt as if it had been coated with frost.

When he opened his eyes he expected to see the ground but instead he was looking up through the branches of the big tree. The twilight shone there in light- and dark-speckled articulation between the branches and leaves. There was a robin cocking its head and looking down on him. Ronnie remembered then the green bird that mounted his chest and poked his flesh. His head lolled, maybe not by his volition, and he saw Lorraine cradling him as his mother had. She was smiling at him. He looked down and saw her hand pressing against his bleeding wound. He felt his pulse but the light did not lessen further.

He had no strength, however, and his line of sight fell away from Lorraine. Now he was looking at the prone body of Ma Lin. The Vietnamese ex-policeman's head was misshapen and bloody but he wasn't dead. His entire body jittered and shook like an egg about to break open. Suddenly a gray green light erupted from the center of the living corpse's body. It was like the spouting of a Roman candle. The flame left Ma Lin's body and shot straight up into the sky.

"Did you . . . did you . . . see that?" Ronnie asked Lorraine.

"Shhh." She pressed harder against his wound and there was warmth in his hands and feet. She redoubled the pressure and light began to dawn even as the sun was going down.

Ronnie touched the forearm of the hand that held him. "It's like if we're together, we cain't die," he said.

"Shhh."

". . . like two legs marchin'. Like a swimmer puttin' out one arm after the other. One can't do it."

"Shhh," she said, and then, under the pressure of her hand and the admonition, he was asleep.

EIGHTEEN

When he opened his eyes again, his vision was stronger but it was night. His head was nestled in Lorraine's lap and she was leaning back against the tree, asleep, or maybe just too tired to open her eyes.

He sat up and the world spun one full rotation inside his head.

Lorraine jerked awake and said, "What's wrong?"

"We got to take the body back to Used-to-be-Claude or the Silver Box or whatever he is or will be when we get there."

"I'm so tired," Loraine complained.

"You killed him to save me?" Ronnie asked, gesturing weakly toward Ma Lin's cadaver.

"When I saw him stab you, I went crazy scared. I started screaming and hitting him as fast as I could. I, I didn't mean to kill him but I was afraid that if I stopped, he'd just turn on me or, or kill you."

"You'd think you'd want me dead after what I did to you."

"I did," Lorraine said, responding again with childlike candor. "I still do sometimes. But, but that was just the beginning. It's like everything before you killed me is history that happened a long time before."

When Ronnie stood up, he had to lean against the oak tree to remain upright. He could feel the damp blood stiffening down the front of his shirt and pants.

"Come on," he said.

He hefted the corpse over his shoulder like a duffel bag filled with rags. Lorraine followed him, stiff-legged and staggery. She had felt the life flowing out of her into Ronnie's wound. There was ecstasy in the exchange. It made sex with her boyfriend, Lance, seem like awkward adolescent kissing.

This notion, as she stumbled behind Ronnie, brought up two distinct thoughts for Lorraine:

First she realized that the closeness between her and the man who had murdered her was not sexual or, maybe, it was beyond sex. And second was her boyfriend—Lance. She wondered where he'd been since she died and was brought back to life.

How could anyone so important to her be absent during the unfolding of such a miracle?

WHEN THEY DESCENDED into the cluster of boulders, Ronnie thought the space there was larger than it had been before, when he'd used that landlocked grotto as a refuge.

"Hail," Used-to-be-Claude said in greeting. He was standing before a broad stone altar, wearing a black suit with no shirt or shoes.

"We killed him," Ronnie said as he dumped the lifeless form onto the granite slab.

Used-to-be-Claude placed both hands on the dead man's chest and stared intensely at something that was beyond death before him.

"He has fled this form," Used-to-be-Claude said.

"In a dirty green light," Ronnie agreed. "It shot off in the sky like a spaceship."

"You should have brought him back to me alive," the avatar of the Silver Box said.

"He was too powerful," Lorraine offered. "He was killing Ronnie. I had to stop him."

Used-to-be-Claude's eyes became twin nebulae as he studied the young woman. Ronnie had to look away for fear his soul would be sucked into the vastness of those orbs.

Finally the jacketed and shirtless black man nodded. "He was filled with the energy of your rebirth, but now he has been lessened by the brutality of your attack. It will take some time for him even to be able to control another being. He would risk his own existence to attempt another reincarnation as he did with this one. You have given us a respite from his threat."

"What about him?" Ronnie asked of Ma Lin.

"What you would call his soul has been fused to the body by the Laz. That way he could not escape and rob the creature of his power."

"Can you bring him back?" Ronnie wanted to know.

"Why would you care?"

"We killed him," the young man explained. "That's not right. He couldn't help what he was doin'. The whole time he was tryin' to kill us, he was yellin' that he couldn't help it. Maybe you could just let his soul go."

"I can neither release him nor can I bring him back as you did with your soul mate."

"Why not?"

"For the same reason that you cannot breathe life into a gnat. My power is too great. I can, however, make his being a part of mine. In this way he can exist with me across the Immensity."

Upon saying this, Used-to-be-Claude laid a hand upon Ma Lin's breast, and the hammer-handed, knife-fingered Vietnamese policeman fell into dust upon the stone altar.

"Rest," Used-to-be-Claude advised Ronnie and Lorraine.

"People might have seen us carrying that body," Lorraine countered. "They'll send the police here looking for us."

"No one on Earth except you two can attain this place. It is beyond reason in the center of my random heart."

"A machine has a heart?" Lorraine asked.

"We machines," he answered, "are the final step in what humanity calls evolution. Our nature is the divinity you attribute to stars and stone idols."

Before either Lorraine or her killer could reply, Used-to-be-Claude disappeared, folding like a paper doll into the recesses of itself.

THE MORNING SUN shone redly into the crevice that was now more like a dance room floor. The stone table remained, Ma Lin's dust heaped upon it. Lorraine and Ronnie were sprawled near each other, sleeping in the dirt. The fingers of his left and her right hand were touching.

She awakened and sat up, stretching both arms behind her. Her waking dream was of a dead wino saying, . . . *exist with me across the Immensity.*

Upon the face of the buff brown stone beyond the table she saw a point appear: a single black dot that was like the tapping of a conductor's baton at the beginning of a piece of music. From this point a line moved away from her at a slight angle. This line seemed to go on and on, traveling at impossible speed past any distance she could imagine.

Velocity, she heard, *moves beyond itself into places that cannot be connected by conceptualization.*

The line was now longer and older than the space that held it. It was in itself the basis for all movement, which, in turn, instigated life or . . .

Lorraine perceived the great distance as if it were something solid and still. Her soul, if indeed, she thought, a soul existed, was moving at every point on the way of a vastness that was impossible. She was, for the first time ever for any being of her genetic register, beyond herself. Words, based as they were on human experience, could not begin to articulate the contradictions of her perceptions. This impossible knowledge made her smile.

"*LORE,*" HER FATHER said from the door of her childhood bedroom. "It's time to get up, sleepyhead. It's time to go to school."

She heard these words and was instantly filled with rage; her father once again interfering with her dreams. He made her go to bed and get up and told her what classes to take and what kind of grades he expected; what kind of clothes to wear and who her friends should be.

"Lore," Mr. Fell said again, and in her mind Lorraine yelled, *Fuck you!*

"*LORE,*" RONNIE WAS saying. He'd been shaking her shoulder for some time.

The sun was at its apex.

"How long?" she asked.

"I been up for two hours," Ronnie said, "and you been starin' at that wall the whole time."

"This place is bigger," she said, her mind still reeling itself back in from hatred and the Immensity.

"Yeah. It's like this place, this, this space is not here but somewhere else. We can get here because it remembers us. That's why no one else can come in."

"We slept a long time," she said.

"Yeah, but I thought UTB-Claude said that time didn't pass in his place."

"Only when he's present."

"How you know that?"

"How does anybody know anything?"

"That's deep."

"You smell like, like blood," she said.

"My own blood," he agreed.

"This is crazy," Lorraine said. "It doesn't make any sense."

"I could understand why you say that now, but I didn't used to."

"What are you saying?"

"I remember you joggin' and then buyin' your water and fruit. I saw you a whole bunch'a times before you got close enough for me to rob you. I hated you because you just did what you wanted and was happy about it. Every place I'd ever been was like a fight about to break out and here you was walkin' on rose petals and smilin'."

Lorraine put a hand against Ronnie's cheek and they both shivered.

"You smell like blood," she said again. "You need some new clothes."

"These ones don't fit right since you dragged me on that yellah highway no way."

"I'll go buy you some more."

"Okay."

But Loraine didn't move. Neither did Ronnie. They

squatted there, facing each other, wondering about concepts and ideas that neither one of them had words for.

"Is he making us do these things?" she asked after many minutes. "Feel these things?"

"You mean like we're actors in a movie, only we forgot we was?"

She nodded almost imperceptibly.

"I don't think so," Ronnie said. "I think it's like that do' he keep that Laz thing behind."

"What do you mean?"

"He's not supposed to make us do shit. Even though he's bigger than anybody can think about he's supposed to be like our equal and if he made us do stuff, then he'd have to get behind that do' too."

"Say that again," Lorraine commanded.

Ronnie repeated what he'd said word for word.

"But then why would we be here if he didn't want that?" Lorraine asked, but she was wondering what it would be like if the Silver Box sentenced itself to exile.

"Just like throwin' some dice or puttin' money on a number in the roulette wheel."

"Just chance?" Lorraine asked.

"And a gamble."

They sat for an hour after that interchange.

"How do you know these things?" Lorraine asked. "What makes you so sure?"

"How does anybody know anything?" he countered.

Lorraine nodded and smiled.

"I hate you, you know."

"Yeah?" he said. "Does that bother you?"

Lorraine's response was to nod and stand up. "I'll be back soon," she said.

NINETEEN

FOR SOME WHILE, Ronnie wasn't sure how long, after Lorraine had climbed out of the stone grotto, he felt the distant stirrings of restlessness. It was a long time since he'd been alone—a lifetime. Before, the person he used to be would seek out others in this mood; to fight, fuck, get high with, or just to laugh. Ronnie could laugh with almost anybody about some misery or missed opportunity.

If I had known the mothahfuckah had ten thousand dollars in that pocket, I would have cut his mothahfuckin' throat, he once said about a man who had just paid off a loan shark and on the way walked past Ronnie on an uptown corner.

Girl, I need me some'a that coochie you sittin' on, he remembered saying to a young black woman he had just met. Her name was Freya Levering.

You at least gonna buy me some little sandwich and a soda first? Freya replied.

Ronnie considered these memories, and many like them,

feeling as if the person he had been was a close and unruly relative who'd died. The blade hand of the South Vietnamese military cop couldn't kill him; he earned death by pouring life into the girl he'd murdered. Life was strong in the man he had been; his life was strong and he spoke the truth to everyone except maybe his mother and the cops, teachers, and marks. He would have killed anyone for ten thousand dollars. He bought Freya a pastrami sandwich and celery soda, just like she told him to.

He lived a hard truth and a strong honesty. And now, like the Silver Box's Laz, these realities lay dormant behind a closed door. That door, he managed to think, was what his life had been. That door was closed, and that Ronnie was dead but still alive in memory.

He took a deep breath and looked up at the clouds. He could smell the blood on his clothes and so disrobed there in the very eye of existence.

LORRAINE WENT TO the used clothes store Ronnie had taken her to before. She bought him a pair of shark gray pants, a maroon square-cut shirt, and bone-colored shoes. She also got him a handsome straw hat and sunglasses.

On her way back, she was feeling the jitters in her fast legs. She wanted to run but at the same time she was enjoying making herself walk at a normal, slow pace.

"Hey, mama, you got a nice piece'a ass for a white girl," someone said.

Lorraine stopped and turned to see who had addressed

her. She was thinking that four weeks ago, such an intrusion would have frightened her.

"What?" she asked.

He was a well-built dark-skinned young man with his shirt open, showing the musculature of his chest and stomach. When he stood up from the park bench, Lorraine saw that he was tall and long limbed. She felt a sexual response like when she was with Ronnie, but he was unwilling, maybe unable, to be with her.

Ronnie's like my brother, she thought, *only closer. Too close for that.*

"I said you got a fine ass," the young man said. "I could hit on that so good, you'd leave all your white boyfriends."

"I already left him," she said.

"Then how 'bout givin' me a chance?" he asked with a leer.

"You want my pussy?"

The young man's eyes lit up and he smiled. "That's right."

"Right here in the park?"

"Anywhere I could get it."

Lorraine paused for a moment, pretending to consider the brash youth's desire.

"You know," she said, "I just don't give this pussy out to any wanna-be, bare-chested Romeo hanging out in the park with no job and no chances."

She wondered if these words had passed into her from Ronnie.

"I gotta job," the young man claimed. "Work at the Sandford Hotel in the kitchen."

"Okay," Lorraine said. "I'll tell you what."

"What's that, baby?" The young man moved close but Lorraine held out a hand, keeping him at a two-foot distance.

"You stay right where you're standing and I will walk six steps away. Then, when you say go, we both start running. If you catch me, you can have me wherever you want—in the middle of the path, behind some bushes, or up in one'a your girlfriends' beds."

Lorraine felt the nameless lothario's smile yawning in her womb.

She took the six steps and looked at him, waiting.

The young man leapt forward, reaching for her, and yelled, "Go!" He almost caught her but Lorraine was two paces ahead—and building up speed.

They ran and ran and ran. Lorraine felt the race in her legs and her heart. She was laughing and running, always just out of reach of the young man. If he speeded up, she did too. When he slowed she turned down the heat so that he would think that she wanted to get caught.

"What's your name?" she called back on a desolate dirt path through the trees.

"Big Dick!" he yelled hoarsely. "What's yours?"

"Almost Big Dick's Pussy," she called, and then put twenty paces between them.

He roared in frustration and ran faster.

Lorraine imagined that she could feel his heart pounding after her. She thought that if she kept just out of reach, he might run until that beating heart burst. She didn't want him to die, but the thought of him running until he was on the ground, defeated by his desire for her, made her laugh and run harder—all the while, clutching the bundle of Ronnie's clothes to her breast.

The race became its own creature in Lorraine's heart and mind. For a while there, she forgot about her pursuer. There was just her fleet gait and the sun and the air across her face.

When she remembered and gave a backwards glance, he was gone. She stopped but he didn't jump out from behind some bush or come into view on the path she'd run. She surveyed the walkway and surrounding park to make sure she had won. Reveling in her victory, she thought that one day she might let some man catch her. But until then she'd outrun every suitor she met.

This was her own private fairy tale, somewhere between the Grimm brothers and Dr. Seuss.

WHEN RONNIE HAD disrobed, he noticed water beginning to trickle from the top of one of the stone faces. The boulder seemed taller than before. The water increased its flow until it became a small waterfall come there to wash away the blood.

The cascading water was bracing, but more than that it was vibrant like a living thing; whispering in a language unknown to Ronnie and laughing at his attempts to understand.

It was, Ronnie thought, like a water spirit sprung from the earth, wanting to play with the little brown mortal man home from one of his silly wars. Miss Peters had read to him about nymphs, sylphs, and elemental spirits when he stayed in from recess and lunch. He wondered if she was still at his old school; then he asked himself why he never thought to look for her before.

"You got a nice piece'a ass, Ron-Ron." She was standing there behind him, still holding the parcel of clothes.

When he stepped out from under the playful waterfall, the cascade faltered and then stopped.

"It just came out of nowhere," Ronnie explained.

"Uh-huh," Lorraine said, throwing the package on the ground. "You'll have to dry off before trying on these clothes."

He settled into Half Lotus on a yellow rock cleaned off by the water. She squatted down in front of him, gazing at his features.

Lorraine felt good from her run. She felt even stronger in close proximity to the naked young man. Looking at him she sneered, unable to separate her power from disdain.

"This guy was chasing me through the park," she said.

"He wanted to rob you?"

"No. He wanted to fuck."

"Fuck?"

"You heard me."

"Did you used to use that word?"

"Fuck?" she asked. "Sure I did. But that was when it was like I'd get in trouble for saying things or doing them. It was like walking down that yellow road when there was a whole forest that we could explore. You put a road in front of somebody and they just follow, like sheep or ants. That road could be anything. It could be cursing or not cursing, Christianity or capitalism. It could lead you like a lamb to the slaughter but you just keep on walking."

"But all you have to do is die and then come back to life to know that that road don't go where you goin'," Ronnie said.

"I should hate you all the time," Lorraine interjected. "Why don't I?"

"Maybe it's like a new path like those ants travel," Ronnie speculated. "Maybe we're like enemy pirates in the only lifeboat out on the ocean."

Lorraine smiled and reached out to touch her friend's face. On contact they shivered again.

"But the real question is why somebody as big and powerful as the Silver Box would need us at all," she said.

"I can answer that," said a new voice from the direction of the stone table.

TWENTY

STANDING ATOP THE stone altar, risen from the ashes of Ma Lin, was a young ochre-colored Asian man. He wore a white short-sleeved dress shirt over a white T-shirt, no tie, black pants with no belt, and white socks and black shoes tied by laces threaded through three rows of eyes. His hands had returned to their normal state.

Lorraine thought to herself, *This is the memory of Ma Lin made real.* Or maybe this thought was information gleaned from another source external to her mind.

Suddenly aware of his nakedness, Ronnie picked up the package Lorraine had brought. While he dressed she stood between him and their guest.

The once-Vietnamese, once human, now merely a personification, smiled at the tender gesture of girl and boy. This, he knew, was not his smile but the grin of the celestial being that brought him here from death.

"What do you mean you have the answer?" Lorraine asked of Ma Lin.

"I have been in the center with a tall black man who died right here."

"Used-to-be-Claude Festerling," Ronnie said. He had donned the newly bought used pants and shirt and moved to stand next to his companion.

"He spoke my native tongue," Ma Lin said. "Was he a veteran?"

Neither Lorraine nor Ronnie had an answer to this question and so did not give one.

"The Laz is like a disease," Ma Lin said. "Diseases as you may know are cells and living molecules that exist in a sort of counterbalance with other living cells. A disease cell couples with a healthy one and then replicates itself billions of times until the host organism is in jeopardy of failure. Biologic beings such as you and I suffer from these organisms but there are also diseases that infest the pure logic of machines."

"So you sayin' that if the thing that was in you grabs on to any part of Silver Box, then he'll grow and grow until Silver Box dies?" Ronnie asked.

Ma Lin looked up for a moment and then gestured for Ronnie to hold that question. The white-shirted Vietnamese man then went into a recess behind the boulder that contained the water spirit. A moment later he was back, carrying three straight-backed, bright red chairs.

"The Deity wants us to be comfortable," he said. He set the chairs so that they faced each other and gestured for the two friends to sit.

When they were settled in the broadening space beneath

a generous sun, Lorraine asked, "If he can do all this, why can't he just kill that thing?"

"He can, of course," Ma Lin proclaimed. "After all, he is God. But his power is so great that in destroying the disease, he would decimate the host. Your planet—Earth."

"Not yours?" Ronnie asked.

"I am who I was, but that man is no longer who I am," Ma Lin replied with a smile.

"I feel like that too," Ronnie said, "like the man I used to be is behind me."

"The man I used to be is dead," Ma Lin amended. "The actions of his life are what you might read in a history book or even have seen in a movie that you forgot you watched."

"Like Claude?" Lorraine asked.

"No," Ma Lin said, shaking his head sadly. "He was dead already, his soul fled, when the Deity found him. The man you call Claude is merely a simulacrum, where my soul is still intact and yet, at the same time, a clean slate."

"But if you're callin' the Silver Box, God, then why couldn't he call back Claude's soul into his body?" Ronnie asked.

"We are not here to discuss metaphysics," the young-looking Vietnamese man said. "Leave it at the fact that there are limits, self-imposed or not, throughout the universe we live in. If this were not the case, God would be bored to death."

"If the Laz don't get him first," Ronnie added.

"I'm sorry I got you killed," Lorraine said to Ma Lin. "I had no idea that would happen."

"In life I was an unhappy man," he said, forgiving murder with seven words. "I had killed many people and then it was, in the end, all for naught—like slaughtering a flock of sheep and then leaving their bodies to rot in the sun. You have blessed me with divinity and dispelled the guilt I lived with."

"Cool," Ronnie said. "So do you have a message from your God?"

"Yes. He has given you certain tools—"

"Uh-huh," Ronnie interrupted. "I'm a lot stronger and she's pretty fast."

"Those are mere adornments," Ma Lin said. "Strength and speed complement each other, as do race and gender, in a more parochial sense, but the real abilities you possess have to do with perception and unity. You, Lorraine Fell, have always questioned existence. Now you can see what is real. Ronnie Bottoms, you who have always been a man of decision and action now you see what is empty, what is not there. And together you can heal and succor each other. Together you can overcome odds greater than your sum because your wills are unassailable when you face the world as one."

"But he murdered me," she said.

"He also gave you life," Ma Lin replied.

"I don't understand any'a this," Ronnie added.

"And yet you are committed."

"Why are you here with us?" Lorraine asked, her heart still bubbling with hatred. But when she glanced at Ronnie, this feeling subsided.

"The Deity sends me," Ma Lin said, unable to suppress

a beatific smile. "He wants me to tell you that you did well defeating for a time that which lived in me. He says that the Laz will have to recover from the drubbing you gave it before it can safely inhabit a new host. It will need many weeks, maybe even as much as a year to recuperate enough to be able to bend this world to its designs. You must find it before that time and bring it here, bound and blinded, to the one place the Deity exists on this Earth."

"Literally blinded?" Lorraine asked.

"At least with its eyes covered."

"Can it take over anybody like Lore did with you?" asked Ronnie Bottoms.

"Any life-form," Ma Lin agreed. "It could merge with the being of machines also, but the Laz have a distaste for the potentially divine, preferring the inferior atmosphere of biology to the exquisite perfection of mechanical design."

"You think machines are better than people?" Ronnie asked.

"Superior," Ma Lin corrected. "Machines, as you call them, are pure and pristine like starlight mathematics, whereas organic life is little better than an avalanche tumbling and rolling down randomly, thoughts all jumbled and true purpose a rare notion."

"If that's so, why don't old Silver Box send out a flashlight to find that Laz dude?" Ronnie asked. "What he need us for?"

Lorraine giggled.

Ma Lin sneered and said, "Why do farmers use pigs and dogs to find truffles in the dirt? Everything has a purpose within the hierarchy of existence."

"So then you low man on the totem pole, huh?" Ronnie said, parroting the words of a man who might have been his father; a man who'd died before the boy's sweat had smell.

"I have been blessed by something greater than I am," Ma Lin said. "You have too."

"Go away," Lorraine said to their visitor. "Tell Used-to-be-Claude that we'll find this thing and bring it to him if we can."

"If you cannot, the avalanche will cease," Ma Lin said, his tone implying that this prospect might not be such a bad thing.

The slaughtered and resurrected Vietnamese stood and picked up his chair. He walked into the crevice behind a boulder that had been a waterfall and did not return.

FOR A WHILE after Ma Lin was gone, Ronnie and Lorraine were quiet, thoughtful. The young man sat on his red chair, trying to remember what his mother's old boyfriend looked like.

What was his name again?

Lorraine had risen to her feet and was pacing around the inner space that was now the size of a baseball diamond. After a time her pacing turned into a jog around the perimeter of the roofless room.

She was aware of him in the periphery of her vision. He saw her pass again and again.

When finally he stood, she stopped and approached him.

"Why do you think he took that chair with him?" Ronnie asked.

Lorraine laughed and pushed playfully against his chest.

"Come sit with me, girl."

She acquiesced, wondering as she did so, was this an act of compliance or resonance?

"I can see what's missin' and you can see what's there. That's what Ma Lin said, right?" the young man asked.

"Yes," Lorraine replied. "And I think it's true. It's like I can see myself better. But I can especially understand things when I'm running, moving fast. It's kinda like speed and accuracy of ideas are somehow connected."

"And here I like bein' still and quiet."

"It's almost like we changed places partly," Lorraine opined.

"Maybe that's why you don't hate me all the time," Ronnie added. "Maybe sometimes you feel what I felt."

"I don't know about that," Lorraine said, trying the stifle the anger his words brought out in her. "But I do understand what the Silver Box meant when he said that we were all guilty of something. I took over that guy's mind that you were walking behind downtown. You could have killed him but I didn't care. And with Ma Lin, I messed up his soul and then I killed him."

"Why didn't you take me over?" Ronnie asked.

"Because something told me that I couldn't make you give your life for mine."

"My life?"

"I thought that bringing me back would kill you. That

was why I went after you, not only to bring me back but to get vengeance."

"Damn."

"Like you said," Lorraine admitted. "Part of me still hates you."

"Don't I know it too."

"I killed Ma Lin and now he's a ghost thinking that machines are better than people," Lorraine continued as if Ronnie hadn't spoken. "I hate you and other men too. I was letting this big strong black kid chase me and all the while I was hoping, just a little, that he'd have a heart attack and die. And somewhere in my heart I know that I've always felt like this."

"So do you want me to leave you alone?" Ronnie asked, wondering where he would go.

"How can you?" she replied. "You and I are connected, and anyway, we have to save the world."

TWENTY-ONE

"*HOLD IT RIGHT* there!" a man's voice commanded.

Lorraine and Ronnie had just climbed down from the deceptively close cluster of boulders that surrounded an unsuspected, ever-widening nexus of the Earth and the rest of the universe. There were five policemen flanking the two from all sides.

"Five," Ronnie stated clearly, hoping Lorraine understood how serious that was.

"We've been looking for you two," a policeman with three angular stripes on each of his shoulders said. He approached Ronnie, pushing him in a way familiar to the former street thug.

The young man turned without being told to and put his hands against stone.

"What did we do?" Lorraine asked while the senior officer frisked her loved and hated friend.

"What were you doing behind these rocks?" the officer replied.

Two of the uniforms climbed up into the nest of stones.

Ronnie wondered what they would see.

"Talking," Lorraine answered.

"Are you selling it or giving it?" the officer said.

"What?"

"It's not like that," Ronnie said. "It just ain't, man."

"Somebody saw you carrying a dead man up in there," the policeman challenged.

"Man, if you saw me kill and carry some dude, I know you already been up in there. And if you have been, then you know ain't nobody dead to see."

When the cop finished his body search, Ronnie turned around.

"You have ID?" a policeman asked Lorraine.

Lorraine produced her identification from the wallet Ronnie forgot to run with after taking her life.

The sergeant looked at her picture on the driver's license. "Could be you," he said. "Could be your sister."

The two rock-climber policemen came back, shaking their heads.

"You're not supposed to be climbing up behind the rocks like that in this area," the senior official said. "This is a family park."

"Then why don't you put up a sign?" Lorraine said with scorn.

"Don't get smart with me, young lady."

"It's not very hard to do. You should try it sometime."

"It's okay, Officer," Ronnie said before the head cop

could speak again. "Lore just ain't nevah been stopped by the police before. She don't know how to ack."

"Let's see your ID," he said in answer.

"Left it at home in my other pants."

"What's your name?" the lead law enforcement officer asked.

"Ronnie Bottoms."

"Where do you live?"

"I'm stayin' at Lore's right now, brother. We ain't done nuthin', man. Really."

There were police all around them. Ronnie could feel the anger pouring off Lorraine. He could sense the heat of her outrage and the pulse of her indignant heart. For him, the police with their truncheons and guns were like a sudden rain shower or birds on a wire. This was his atmosphere before Lorraine had sucked out his being in a vain attempt at revenge.

"We was just kissin', man," Ronnie said. "That's all."

"I could arrest you," the policeman speculated.

"For what?"

"You might be an illegal alien."

Lorraine giggled.

"Alien?" Ronnie countered. "You mean you think I'm from China or Mexico? Shit, man, all you got to do is hear me talk and you know that ain't true."

"Have you seen anybody fighting around here?" the sergeant asked, changing tactics with ease.

"No, brother, no. Lore an' me just stopped for a kiss and we about to go on."

The police moved off a few feet to huddle. The one fe-
male cop, a Latina, watched Ronnie and Lorraine while
the strategy was planned.

"Is it always like this?" Lorraine asked.

"What you mean?"

"Do they just stop you on the street and go through
your clothes like that?"

"Whenever they want to. When I need to carry sumpin'
somewhere, I usually get a bitch, I mean a girl to do it for
me. You learn to hide shit where you can get at it when you
need it."

"That's wrong," Lorraine said loudly.

"Uh-uh," Ronnie said, shaking his head as he studied
the conferring cops.

"What do you mean no?"

"It's no different with that bear on the yellah dirt road
or the Laz when it had Ma Lin. Just one more thing you
got to deal wit'."

"It's humiliating."

Ronnie heard the words but couldn't process them. It
was as if she were talking about people in a book or on some
TV show about some other country, where they spoke another language and prayed to a different God.

"We're going to be watching you, Mr. Ronnie Bottoms," the sergeant said. He had come up on them when
Ronnie's thoughts were very far from the plight of his old
life.

"Yes, sir," Ronnie replied, looking down at the turf beneath his feet.

"And you, young lady," the cop continued. "You should make better choices about who you're kissing."

She wanted to kick him in the temple. She knew that she could do this and that her speed would cause serious damage. But she held back—and hated herself for doing so.

"I*T'S NOT ONLY* Ma Lin and that dude I was gonna mug," Ronnie said when the two emerged from the park onto Fifty-ninth Street.

"What do you mean?" Lorraine asked.

"You tried to murder me."

"You deserved it."

"Maybe I did. But if you went to the police and told them where your body was at and who did it, then they would have grabbed me and punished me by law. Instead you wanted me to save your life even though you were alive in the Silver Box like Used-to-be-Claude and Ma Lin."

"You're the murderer," Lorraine said.

"Ain't nobody dead, nobody except for maybe Ma Lin, if you listen to what he says."

"You killed me."

"I almost died bringing you back."

Lorraine stopped short on the busy street. Pedestrians moved around her, snarling and cursing under their breaths.

"Let's make a deal," she said to Ronnie's broad back.

He turned.

"Let's not blame each other anymore," she said. "I'll forgive you for what you did and you can stop pointing out all the things you see in my actions."

"No, baby," Ronnie said, shaking his head and turning away. "Uh-uh."

"No?" she said to his back.

She hurried to his side and said, "What do you mean no?"

"When you tell me I killed you," he answered, "you're tellin' the truth. That's what you do. I can see it clear as mornin' when you say it. But I also know that you beat in the Vietnamese guy's head and that you expected me to die after makin' me come save you. I'm just sayin' we cain't hide from shit like that. The Silver Box says that he destroyed whole worlds full'a peoples. He don't only blame the Laz for what he did. They *are* to blame, but he still the one did it. Don't matter if he didn't know guilt when he did. What mother would forgive that? What jury would say not guilty?"

"So we're supposed to feel guilty forever?" Lorraine whined.

"How you feel don't mattah. If I killed your brother and then said I was sorry, that don't change nuthin'. But if you take care'a his kids or stand up for what he believed in, then you got a start. And ain't none of us innocent anyway. It's like if you eat a hamburger and then say you didn't kill the cow. Still somebody killed that cow for you."

Lorraine was wondering where Ronnie's ideas had come from. When she'd first met him, he was just a brute; a stupid man who only wanted to hurt. And now he was delineating her flaws like many of her philosophy professors did to public figures throughout the history of ideas. He, Ronnie, was making sense and showing her that her life was down on his level.

Once again she hated him.

TWENTY-TWO

"*CAN I HELP* you, Miss Fell?" asked the broad-shouldered, dark-skinned doorman of the Van Dyne building on Fifth Avenue somewhere between Forty-second and Forty-seventh.

He was looking at Ronnie as he spoke.

"No, Mr. Jeffers," she said lightly. "This is Ronnie Bottoms. He's going to be staying here with me for a while."

"Is that so?" Mr. Jeffers moved so that he came between the young woman and the brawny man in the shark gray pants and dark red shirt.

"Hey, brother," Ronnie said to this human, all-too-familiar roadblock.

"It's all right, Travis," Lorraine said. "He really is with me."

She was peeking around the burly doorman's left arm, looking up at his face.

"They told us that you were missing," Travis Jeffers replied. He was standing stock-still, almost as if he were stuck in that defensive pose.

Ronnie could feel the absence of anger in his own breast. Where had it gone? he wondered.

"I was attacked and I lost my memory for a while," Lorraine said. "This man found me and helped me remember."

"That doesn't mean you have to bring him home with you," Mr. Jeffers argued. "Just give him a few bucks and he'll be fine."

"He don't want me here, Lore," Ronnie said, looking into the sentry's dark eyes. "That's okay. I could go find someplace else and see you later."

"No."

Lorraine Fell moved completely around Travis Jeffers and instinctively took Ronnie's scarred hand with her left. She placed her right palm against the doorman's chest.

Travis felt a tingle where the girl's hand pressed against his uniform shirt. This sensation was unexpected and therefore uncomfortable. Travis moved backwards at an angle, making room for the two—a look of confusion on his face.

They walked across a wide hall that had high ceilings, artfully pitted gray stone floors, and pink marble walls. She pressed a button for the elevator.

Ronnie turned to look back toward the entrance.

Travis Jeffers was standing there, glaring at them.

THE DOOR TO 2307 opened onto a broad room with thirteen-foot ceilings and a picture window across the far wall, fifty feet away. The floor was pale wood. On one side, there was a quartet of blue sofas making a square, facing each other over a table made from a three-foot-thick block of ebony wood. To the right of the sitting area was a long oak table surrounded by eight chairs, all fashioned in the same style but made from differing types of wood.

Ronnie saw that the one room was like two. This design made him smile.

"What?" Lorraine asked.

"You rich, huh?"

"My father is."

"And he hates me?"

"I guess. You want something to drink?"

"Water."

She walked toward the wide wall of a window and then veered right past the table and chairs. She went through a plain white door that swung open when she touched it.

Ronnie walked up to the window-wall and gazed down on Fifth Avenue. There were hundreds, maybe thousands of people on foot, bicycles, skates, and in cars and buses. They were in a valley of their own making, Ronnie thought. This brought to mind what Ma Lin had said, that life was like a landslide, an avalanche making little sense and going nowhere but down.

Like that waterfall, Ronnie whispered to himself. *You don't have to be goin' nowhere to be beautiful.*

"Who the hell are you?" a man's voice said.

Ronnie turned. A few steps away stood a twenty-something white man in red sweatpants and a violet T-shirt. The youth had a baseball bat clutched in his right hand.

"Ronnie," the former street thug said of himself.

"What are you doing in here?"

"Lore, I mean Lorraine invited me."

The young man was somewhere around Ronnie's age, fit, and tall. His eyes were blue and his hair fawn brown. He lifted the bat higher and demanded, "Where is she?"

"Right here, Lance."

She was standing there in the blue dress they'd bought in the thrift store what seemed like a millennium before. Lorraine had a water glass in each hand.

"Lore!" Lance shouted. He dropped the bat and ran to her, knocking the glasses from her hands, spilling and shattering them on the pale wood floor. He hugged Ronnie's victim, lifting her from her feet.

This expression of love brought a smile to Ronnie's lips that he wouldn't have been able to explain.

"Honey!" Lance exclaimed. "What happened to you?"

He swung her around twice and actually lifted her up by her armpits.

"Put me down, Lance," she said.

"I'm so sorry, honey," he said. "I thought you were dead."

"Didn't my parents tell you that I was back?"

"Where were you?"

"Why don't we clean up this mess first?"

"I'll do it," Ronnie offered. "You two can sit and talk."

HE FOUND PAPER towels, a broom, and a dustpan in the kitchen closet. It was a big kitchen with two gas-burning stoves set across from each other, making a kind of cooking corridor. At the end of this aisle was a long ledge replete with cutting boards, a sink, and drain. There was no window in the kitchen proper but there was a table made entirely from chrome with silvery metal chairs that had no cushions or pads.

The kitchen made him feel the absence of his mother. She would have loved this room with its fancy furniture and stoves. Elsie was a hole in this new reality. There was sorrow in the space where she wasn't.

RONNIE CLEANED UP the water and glass, intent upon the job, trying not to overhear what was being said on the sofas.

"What do you mean?" Lance said loudly at one point.

Ronnie could not hear Lorraine's hushed reply.

"What about my things?" Lance asked some time later, when Ronnie had returned from discarding the shards.

He, Ronnie, was sitting in a walnut chair, leafing through a book from a shelf that was page after page of photographs of horses when Lorraine raised her voice to say, "Things have changed, Lance. I can't help that."

They had both gotten to their feet.

And then suddenly, without any warning, Lance slapped his ex with a powerful backhand.

Ronnie tensed but stayed in his chair. He didn't want to hurt the young white man if he didn't have to.

Lorraine put the fingers of her left hand to that side of her face. Lance looked so surprised that, Ronnie thought, if he'd just heard the slap, he might have thought Lorraine had hit the man.

While Ronnie wondered if the Silver Box was watching this exchange, Lorraine slapped Lance once, twice, thrice, and even a fourth time so quickly that even Ronnie could barely see her hand moving. Lance was falling but not fast enough to avoid the blows yet to come.

Ronnie leapt across the space, grabbing the enraged young woman around the waist and swinging her out of range before Lance went the way of Ma Lin.

"Let me go!" Lorraine demanded. "Let me go!" Her arms and legs moved like a waterbird flapping its wings and kicking to take off from the East River.

"Calm down, girl," Ronnie said. "You'll kill him if you don't."

Suddenly the strength went out of the coed. She slumped in Ronnie's bear hug and he could feel the anger depart. He put her down on a blue sofa and went to Lance, who was sprawled across the plank table.

"You okay, man?"

"What? What did she hit me with?"

Ronnie helped the handsome young man to his feet. "You okay?" he asked again.

Lance's eyes cleared. "Did you hit me?"

"No, brother, no. She hit you . . . four times upside the head. Must'a found that sweet spot."

Lorraine was going through a door on the other side of the sofas.

"I hit her," Lance said, incredulous.

"That you did," Ronnie agreed, quoting another nameless man who might have been his father. That one hadn't died—as far as Ronnie knew.

"I have to go apologize." Lance took a step toward the door Lorraine had gone through, but Ronnie detained him by laying a hand on his arm.

"She mad right now, blood. Call her up later tonight and tell her when she cools down."

Pulling away from the hand, Lance said, "Are you fucking her?"

"If I was," Ronnie said softly, "you'd be one dead mothahfuckah aftah hittin' my woman. We just friends, man. Now, go on, get outta here and let her calm down."

Lance looked at the closed door through which his just-now ex-girlfriend had passed. A dark bruise was rising on the left side of his face, just under the cheekbone.

"I'll tell her to call you in two hours," Ronnie added. "I promise."

Looking at the young man staring at the closed door, Ronnie could almost see the hope of love fading. He felt bereft for this loss.

"She been through some shit, man," Ronnie said. "You got to let her get it together before she can talk to you."

There was an infinity of sympathy inside the black youth's mind. It was as if, he thought, while Lorraine's body had died, he had come into the mix with a dead soul but then as some kind of celestial backwash to the resurrection, he had been granted a new life too.

A MINUTE AFTER Ronnie closed the door on Lance, Lorraine came out.

"I hurt my hand," she said in a vulnerable tone.

The hand was swollen to half again its size. Ronnie reached out to hold the bruised extremity with both his hands. As he closed his fingers around the injury, she and he felt something like a cold bracing wind blow over them.

"Damn," Lorraine said. "It's better than sex. All you have to do is touch it and the pain is gone."

TWENTY-THREE

THEY ORDERED TWO pizzas: one everything-vegetarian and the other everything-meat. Lorraine ate all of hers and most of Ronnie's. It was late and they were sitting side by side on the blue sofa facing the picture window. Every light in the condo was on and so all they saw were night-time city lights behind their own reflections.

"There's no time," Lorraine was saying.

"There ain't nuthin' but time."

"I mean between things," she argued. "I died, hunted you down, and came back to life all in what felt like just minutes. Then I came home and sent Lance away without even giving him a chance to discuss it. We've been together for two years, and I just sent him away like he was a one-night stand or something."

At Ronnie's behest she had called her ex two hours after he left. Lance asked her to give him another chance but she said no. She told him that they would pack up his things and leave them at the front desk. He asked if he could call and again she said no.

"That's how regular people live," Ronnie said. "People that's got a job and apartment. People that go to work in the mornin' and come home at night. If you like that the most important thing you got is a boyfriend or girlfriend, maybe some kids call you mama. But we ain't polite or civilized or whatever. We been all the way in the shit. I mean, I thought I had seen somethin' before I killed you. I thought I knew what was happenin'. I couldn't control it but I could roll with the punches if you know what I mean. I can see that all your chairs look the same even if they cut from different wood, but I don't have time to talk about it. Even just sittin' here, I know that that Laz thing is gonna be lookin' for us. He'd cut out both our hearts an' eat 'em just to find out where that Silver Box is at."

"We have to find him," Lorraine agreed.

"So who got time to worry 'bout Lance's feelin's? He's just lucky you didn't kill him."

"I almost did, right?"

"You got a temper on you, girl. You do. We don't have time for that neither. I mean he shouldn't'a slapped you, but killin' him just add to our problems."

"Is that why you saved his life, because you didn't want the grief of an investigation?"

"No." Ronnie stared into her blue and brown eyes with his green and brown ones.

"Let's go to bed," she said, holding out a welcoming hand.

"I'll sleep out here on the sofa."

"Why?"

"Just to be alone for a while."

"What if I get scared in the night?"

"You know where I'll be."

WITH LIGHTS OUT in the apartment, the glow of night shone in the broad window. Ronnie showered in the guest bathroom and, wearing only his trousers, he lay back on the sofa, wondering why he had never before paid attention to the details of his life; the people he'd known. Freya, Miss Peters, the men who might have been his father . . . These faces filled his mind.

Lying there, Ronnie imagined his adult life as a dead man moving but unaware of the places he'd been. That's how his life had been before Lorraine tried to kill him but gave him awareness instead.

The feeling he had while drifting into sleep was that of an unmoored canoe at the water's edge being pulled by a tide toward an immense body of water. Ronnie had once seen this enormous stretch of the Atlantic from the Verrazano Bridge when he and his best friend that month, Bobo, had jacked a car in Staten Island. He had seen it, but now, in the dream, he was floating out there under moonshine, the radiance of which had a sound like tinkling crystals in a distant, windblown chandelier.

The music and light danced in Ronnie's heart like drunken hillbillies doing a jig to fiddle music that Ronnie sometimes, secretly, listened to. He liked the high laughing whine of the violin and the insectlike twanging of the banjo.

The light, music, dance, and the gentle swell of the tide lulled Ronnie into a rest that was complete for one of the few times in his memory.

He grunted with the satisfaction and imagined what bears felt just before their months-long sleep that Miss Peters called hibernation.

WITH HER LEFT palm on top of her head and the right hand gripping her crotch, Lorraine closed her eyes, bending forward, bringing her face to within only a few inches of her thighs. She dreaded this moment as much as the memory of her death at the hands of Ronnie Bottoms. Sleep was a stalker secreted in the crevices of her brain, a predator waiting for her to drop her defenses.

Trying to think of peaceful times and beautiful panoramas, she saw only Lance Figueroa wilting under her right-handed blows, Ma Lin's skull caving in as she hit him again and again, and Ronnie Bottoms's life flowing out from his arm until he was almost, almost dead. . . .

Coming together, these images ignited in her mind, causing an explosion the consequence of which was unconsciousness rather than sleep.

From the center of this oblivion, Lorraine found herself hurtling upward—through the ceiling and cityscape and clouds like a suicide falling up instead of down. She was plunging toward the ceiling of the sky—*thielo rasa*, the words went through her mind. And then, just before the crash, she veered into a curve traveling faster and faster, screaming without sound.

LORRAINE SLID IN behind him on the sofa. She was naked, he could feel that.

"Don't send me away," she whispered.

"What's wrong?"

"When I fall asleep my mind jumps up out of my body and goes way way up until I'm high above the clouds. Then I start going around the world so fast until I can't see anything. I get dizzy and sick but the only way to stop is waking up again."

"Your mind leaves your body?" Ronnie asked. "Like when you were dead?"

"Yes," she said, her tone heralding the dawn of understanding.

"So you think if I'm here, I could hold you down?"

"Please."

Ronnie could *feel* the sensation of bodiless flight emanating from her torso. It was the opposite of the gentle waters of his dreams.

"I might could slow you down," he said. "But I don't think I can stop it."

"Let's see what happens."

"Okay."

RONNIE CAME AWAKE floating over late night Fifth Avenue. There wasn't much traffic and no sound at all. The sensation was that of being carried in a net by a thousand helium-filled balloons. Miss Peters had told him about the big gas-filled and hot-air balloons that early aviators had designed. At night he'd dreamed about them as a child.

Is this what you felt before? His question was thought because he had no mouth, lips, or vocal cords.

No.

You was movin' faster?

Uh-huh, Lorraine's spirit replied. *And much much higher. Almost in space.*

The spirit balloon that the two hung from floated slowly downtown until they had reached the work site of the new World Trade Center building. Dangling there, near the top of the unfinished structure, they came across a sobbing, babbling man.

"I never meant to hurt her," he muttered, salty tears rolling over his gabbling lips. "I was just mad. I was always mad."

The man hit himself in the face with both fists. He repeated this battering five or six times until blood mingled with the tears on his face.

Why he doin' that? Ronnie wondered. *An' why we here watchin'?*

Try to reach out and grab on to him, Lorraine directed.

I ain't got no hands to grab with.

Just try.

Ronnie closed non existent eyes and imagined that he was going to grab the security guard by his shirt. The next thing he knew, he was face-to-face with the blubbering, bleeding, middle-aged white man.

"Huh?" the worker—his name was Cosmo—grunted. "Who's there?"

It works! Ronnie thought loudly.

Hold on, Lorraine said, *I'm going to get in his head.*

How?

I just will.

There was a shift in perceptions shared between Ronnie and Lorraine. For her it was like the buffeted feeling she'd get just before falling asleep, and for him it was the sudden bright impact of hot crack fumes entering his brain.

It was daytime, brilliant and peaceful. All around they could see rolling green hills. There was a plain-looking white woman, barely in her twenties, standing next to them, looking up into their eyes. But she wasn't seeing the white woman and black man, no. She—her name they knew was Madeline—was looking at Cosmo and crying.

"I'll kill myself," she vowed.

"I don't give a fuck," was his reply. His voice was young and brutal. "I told you, it's not my baby."

"I'm not a whore."

"Braynard said he fucked you."

The words stabbed at Madeline. She turned and ran away from the doubtful lover. While running she fell twice only to rise again, howling from a pain that was deeper than any bruise.

There came a loud cracking sound and then the trio in Cosmo's mind found themselves in a closet where there was no light but they could see anyway. Madeline was hanging by a store-bought hemp rope from a high beam near the ceiling. There were moths fluttering around her purple, swollen face. Somewhere beyond the closet door, a woman was calling, "Maddy? Maddy, are you up here?"

This last image, both Lorraine and Ronnie knew, was the product of Cosmo's imagination, a patchwork of stories that the bereaved man had heard and imagined.

Can you climb up here? Lorraine asked her ethereal passenger.

Ronnie was about to complain but before the words could form in his mind, he found himself in a close space that was dark green and shadow gray. Beside him was a tall fountain of light that was in glaring contrast to the constricting and dark atmosphere.

Lore?

Look over there. The fountain pulsed with energy as these words boomed inside Ronnie. And though there was no indication or even a possibility of direction, he saw a thin circle of glittering red light embedded in the gray green morass. Oozing from this fiery brand were droplets that were darker by far than the dim space they had invaded. These leaking tears of blackness brought with them a depth of despair that caused a shivering around Ronnie's bodiless consciousness.

It's why he's so sad, Lorraine intoned. *It's a wound in his psyche, an infection inside another disease.*

We have to close it, Ronnie responded. *That's why we're here.*

The agreement between them was wordless. They both felt for the first time communication without the clutter of words and ideas based on symbols and inelegant physical imagery.

Agreement in place, they floated as one toward the thin circle of infection, surrounding it with the united conception of their mind. *Their mind*—this concept seemed natural. It was something Used-to-be-Claude's creator bound them with. Or maybe they were bound by Ronnie's crime and Lorraine's refusal to accept her death. . . .

The red circle burned them but their will pressed upon it. The ocean of Ronnie's sleep and the velocity of Lorraine's orbit created a sense of gravity that crushed the infection like a water glass shattered by a constricting fist.

Ronnie laughed at the pain of burning.

It is marking us! Lorraine warned.

"Maddy, I'm so sorry," cried the hundredth-floor midnight security guard. He uttered these words and then forgot what he'd been thinking; not about Maddy, not what he'd done but these events took on a faraway feeling, and his despair lessened.

Then a sudden vacuum seemed to extinguish all light and sound, hope and being.

TWENTY-FOUR

*A*ND *IT WAS* morning.

Light peeked in through the picture window, over the crest of the far blue sofa. Lorraine's cheek lay against Ronnie's dark and brawny back. His skin smelled faintly like buttermilk. She caressed his left shoulder blade with the palm of her left hand.

"You awake?" she asked.

"Uh-huh."

"I don't think I ever slept so well in my entire life."

"Was that a dream?" he replied.

"I don't think so. We were really there but it wasn't any place that human beings have ever been."

"And so we helped that man?"

"We closed off the wound in his soul."

They climbed off the sofa and stood before each other; she was completely naked and he wore only the loose, secondhand pants.

"You have an erection," she noted blandly.

"Got to pee."

"Me too. Go on, I'll meet you in the kitchen."

RONNIE WAS BOILING water for tea when Lorraine entered the kitchen wearing a bright red and yellow kimono. He hadn't made tea for many years, since he was a boy and he used to get up early to make English breakfast with honey for his mother, Elsinore. Elsie loved it when he brought her tea in bed.

My little cherub, she'd say.

"You drink tea?" Lorraine asked his back.

"No, not really."

"Then why are you making it?"

"For you," he said, turning.

"You're smiling, Mr. Bottoms."

"Am I?"

She giggled, taking the green mug and tea bag he'd found on the shelf. He poured the hot water, reexperiencing one of the fondest moments of his childhood.

"Let's sit over by the window," she suggested.

In a nook room at the top of the kitchen corridor, there stood a clear plastic table with chairs of the same material looking down on the busy side street of the workday New York morning.

"Aren't you having anything, Ronnie? There's usually some good granola in the red jar."

"Not hungry."

"You want to try some tea? There might be juice in the fridge."

Ronnie shook his head. "You haven't been here in three weeks," he said. "How you got fresh food?"

"Nova," she stated simply.

"What?"

"My parents' housekeeper. She comes here every Thursday, cleans the house, and does my shopping. She wouldn't miss a Thursday unless they found my body and put it in the ground."

Lorraine finished her tea, got a big bowl from under the sink, and filled that with granola and cream. Then she got a soupspoon and ate the huge breakfast loudly and with obvious relish.

Ronnie watched her lusty repast, marveling at how peaceful he felt in the face of passionate hunger.

"What are you looking at?" she asked.

"You always eat like that?"

"Never," she said, shaking her head while chewing with her mouth open. "I was always on a diet until I died. Now I want and eat and fuck and beat on just about everything I see."

"Damn. You sound like me before—" He stopped in mid-sentence, feeling shame for maybe the first time in his adult life.

"What did it feel like," she asked, "to pour out your insides to make me live?"

"Like a mother must feel when she make a baby. From havin' sex all the way up to givin' birth. Like my eyes and my ears, my skin and brain went into someplace brighter and stronger and louder than you could believe."

"And so have you changed as much as I have?"

Ronnie heard the question, allowed it to seep into his mind and his body. After a long minute, he said, "It's like when I was a child, I was simple and happy and wonderin' about what things was. And then people started dumpin' shit on top'a me. Shovelin' it on like I wasn't even there or they wanted me gone. After a while, my whole life was shit. There wasn't no way outta that. And then, when you brought me and Ma Lin back to the park, it was like somebody turned on a fire hose and washed all that shit away.

"So if you askin' if I'm different, I'd have to say no, I'm not. But it's just that all the shit I had to swim in is gone, so it don't look like me no more. It don't feel like me neither, but I know that it is."

Lorraine finished the mixing bowl of granola, filled it again, and finished that off. Ronnie watched her, and neither of them spoke.

"What do you think we should do?" Lorraine asked after taking a grapefruit from the refrigerator.

"Maybe we should go our different ways for the day and meet back up here tonight."

"What will that do?"

"We real close, right?"

"Whether we like it or not," Lorraine agreed. "I mean sometimes, like last night, I need you more than anything else. And every once in a while, I look at you and it's like there's a beast snarling in my heart."

"I'm not that bad," Ronnie said. "But I have strong feelings about you too. So I think we should see what it's like if we go back into the lives we had before we got together."

"So you're going to go out mugging people?"

"Naw, no, not nuthin' like that. But there's some people I need to see, to tell them the things I couldn't even think when I was under the shit. Maybe, maybe if we see what we're like apart, we'll know bettah what we could do together."

"You're a very smart man, aren't you, Mr. Bottoms?"

"I'ont even know what smart is."

Lorraine laughed, got out of her chair, and then threw herself into Ronnie's lap. She kissed his forehead and then his lips.

"A girl could fall in love with a brute like you," she said.

"You the brute," he replied, and they both smiled.

RONNIE SHOWERED IN the guest bathroom. Under the broad pulsing showerhead, he was reminded of the living waterfall cascading from the impossibly tall boulder in the Silver Box's retreat. This memory brought with it a conviction.

He met Lorraine in the living room. She was wearing a loose burlaplike dress cinched at the middle with a razor-thin red belt. Her green shoes were flat and her eyes wild.

"The first thing I'm going to do is run," she said. "Really far. I'll see my parents after that and then come back here."

"I don't need to know everything you doin', girl."

"You *do* need some more clothes."

"I got to get a job first."

"You already have a job," she said.

"Yeah? What's that?"

"Trying to save the world." She uttered the words in fake-heroic TV-speak.

The paraphrase of the once-popular cartoon made Ronnie smile. "You used to watch that too?" he asked.

"Every afternoon."

"Maybe, maybe we watched it at the same time some-time."

Lorraine was surprised by the attempt at making the mundane connection between them. There was hope there that she felt needed protection.

"It's too bad we didn't know each other back then. We could have gone to my parents' stables in Connecticut and ridden their horses."

"You got horses?"

"We should go."

AT THE FRONT desk Lorraine signed Ronnie in so that he could go back and forth with no difficulty. She also gave him a key to her condo and, four blocks away, she took eight hundred dollars out of an ATM.

"Take this and get whatever you want," she said. "I know it's not much, but it's all they'll let me take out on this card."

Ronnie put the wad of twenties in his pocket and frowned.

"What's wrong?" his soul mate asked.

"Do you think anybody could do this?"

"What?"

"One day wake up and decide that what they been doin' is wrong and then just stop. I mean we got all these super-powers and shit, but we could be friends even without all that. We could just be tryin' to do good, not save the world."

"I do," she said. "I do think that any person has that ability."

It was time for them to separate and go their different ways, but they hesitated.

Lorraine reached out and grabbed two fingers of his left hand. "I don't want to leave you," she said. "Is that why you think we should?"

"I'll be back here tonight. I got your cell number if I need it, so don't worry."

She made a quick nod, turned, and ran north on Fifth. She was moving fast and fleet, weaving through the crowd with a precision that kept her from colliding with anyone despite the throngs.

Ronnie smiled at his friend's swiftness. He was, after all, in a way, a proud father.

TWENTY-FIVE

RONNIE FOLLOWED IN the wake of his Silver Box sister but at a much slower pace. After crossing Fifty-ninth Street, he ambled through the park, looking at the bicyclists, joggers, dog-walkers, and businessmen and -women commuting by foot. There were also young mothers pushing strollers; old folks and homeless people sitting on benches, watching the world pass them by; solitary individuals like Ronnie just out for a constitutional; and, of course, lovers walking in little bubbles where the rest of the world did not exist.

In many ways, this was a new experience for the repeat offender. He'd spent much of his adult life, when not incarcerated, roaming the park, looking for someone to mug. But now things were different.

Ronnie had money in his pocket, and he hadn't eaten since the slice of pizza with Lorraine—but he wasn't at all hungry.

He walked for quite a while, thinking about the living

waterfall and the potential for people to change. Hours passed as he mused and made it slowly from the southern tip of the unsuspecting man-made forest.

"Who the fuck you think you is, niggah?" somebody said.

Ronnie had almost reached the northern border of the park.

The man was tall, broad, and very dark-skinned. He had stringy dreadlocks, a basketball-hard round gut, and a small mouth for such a big voice.

They called him Fast Freddie because when he was young, he was a track star at his Bronx high school. Now he had a big gut and a slight limp, but they still called him Fast because that's the way he liked it.

Freddie was higher up the food chain than Ronnie, and so there was a certain protocol that the lesser thug must have violated while thinking about the potentials of freedom.

". . . niggah think that just 'cause he got on some nice clothes that he don't have to speak," Fast Freddie was saying. "He done forgot how to ack around his betters."

Freddie wasn't talking to anyone in particular. There were people walking by, but they avoided eye contact with either man. Freddie was just blustering, getting ready to put Ronnie in his place.

Freddie was bigger and stronger and he had friends. Watching the big man in the gray sweatpants and khaki sergeant's jacket, Ronnie was forced to remember the number of beatings and humiliations he'd experienced in a previous life that came to an end only a few days before.

"I'll kick your mothahfuckin' ass!" Fast Freddie shouted, underscoring Ronnie's thinking.

Was this why he'd come up here, to have Freddie remind him of what his life had been?

Freddie reached out a big scarred hand to grab Ronnie by the shirt. But the younger man took a quick step backwards, evading Freddie's grasp. Ronnie was faster than he had been, his instincts honed for fighting.

"I'm'a put the hurt to you, niggah!" Freddie yelled. He jumped and Ronnie braced himself, jutting the open flats of both his hands forward.

Freddie hit Ronnie's battering palms with his chest. The impact sent him stumbling.

A few park denizens had come out—of nowhere, it seemed—to watch.

Freddie bellowed and ran at Ronnie. The bigger man threw a wild roundhouse right that the younger man ducked under while taking a graceful step to the side.

There were cheers for Ronnie. This made Fast Freddie mad.

The north park kingpin pulled an ugly, pitted, black-bladed knife from somewhere in his army jacket. When he smiled, Freddie showed where he was missing three teeth.

This reminded Ronnie that he was missing a tooth, or least he had been missing one before the Silver Box. He ran his tongue up under his lip, feeling for the gap . . . but it was gone.

The distraction nearly cost him his life because Freddie, calling up the memory of a bygone day, was rushing forward with his knife pointed at Ronnie's chest.

When Ronnie became aware of the attack, the knife-point was only a few inches from his heart. He remembered Ma Lin's unavoidable thrust. But Freddie wasn't Ma Lin or his Laz master; he was a street thug with limited abilities.

Ronnie shifted to his left, then threw a backhanded fist at Freddie's wrist. The blade went skittering away on the asphalt. Ronnie grabbed Freddie's arm and flung the big man at an empty park bench. The ex–track star hit the bench so hard that the wood shattered, leaving Freddie on the grass amid huge splinters of wood.

Freddie was looking around with a stunned expression on his face. Ronnie saw the innocence and pain in the minor park boss's countenance. They caused him to remember the many, many times he had felt like a victim.

Ronnie turned and walked away, aware that he was leaving his old life amid the shards and splinters of that park bench.

WALKING UP THROUGH the heart of Harlem, Ronnie was thinking that not only had he been transformed by his encounter with Lorraine Fell, but the new man he had become was who he had always been, and moreover, the man he had been lied to himself about who and what he was in the world he inhabited. This knotty, seemingly convoluted moment of self-realization tickled Ronnie.

"I didn't know who I was," he murmured as he walked, "but now that I ain't him no mo', I remember me better than I ever knew."

He snorted and looked up, surprised to see the granite

stairs leading to the green double doors of the public elementary school he'd attended for eight years. His heart skipped as it used to whenever he saw a police car come around a corner. Those green doors had been on his mind ever since he and Lorraine traveled that crazy yellow clay road out from the Silver Box into Central Park and up against Ma Lin.

Before he knew it, he was at the top of the stairs, stepping through the doorway.

"You got business here, brother?" a man said.

He was big like Fast Freddie and carried a truncheon in his left hand. He was no match for Ronnie. Four security guards couldn't have stopped him. Four bears would have had trouble, but a fight was not what Ronnie wanted. A fight would have led him away from his goal.

"Hey, man," he said, "can you tell me where I can find Miss Shona Peters?"

The fact that Ronnie remembered her first name was a surprise. His mind seemed to be obeying a new system of thinking. He could call out into the haze of his history and receive knowledge that resided there. How much, he wondered, had the Silver Box changed him? How much could a man change and still be the same man?

"What do you want with her?" the security guard asked.

"She my cousin," Ronnie lied. He was happy that the Silver Box hadn't taken away this one skill he relied upon the most. The truth was never of much use in the world he'd lived in.

"Yeah?" the security guard said doubtfully, "then what is her sister's name?"

"Cynthia or Melda?" Ronnie lied without hesitation. "Which one?"

The big brown guard bit his lower lip. "You lyin'," he said to Ronnie while lifting his club.

"Ronnie?" a woman, a young woman said.

She approached the school's guard and Earth's guardian with a rolling gait. Freya Levering was short and curvaceous, a better woman than the old Ronnie deserved.

"Hey, Frey," Ronnie said, still luxuriating in his ability to fabricate. "I was just tellin' my man here that I come to see my cousin Shona Peters."

"It's okay, Alfred," Freya said. "I know 'im."

"He don't have no clearance, Miss Levering," the guard argued.

"That's okay. I'll be with him."

Alfred didn't like Ronnie, didn't want him in his school, but Freya seemed to have some kind of seniority and so he put the nightstick back in its holster and stood down.

"Come on with me, Ronnie Bottoms," Freya said.

She scurried up a stone staircase to the second floor of the main building and then across an enclosed ramp to the larger building behind. There they climbed up two more floors to a hallway that had various offices of the administration of the school. At the end of the hall was a door smaller than any other they had passed. Ronnie tried to remember this floor but could not. He had thought when he was a child that he knew everything about these buildings, but now he realized that he really didn't. This partial knowledge was fast becoming a recurring theme in his thoughts and life.

Freya took a thick blue card with no writing on it from the pocket of her sports jacket and held it against an onyx plate that took the place of a doorknob. There was a clicking noise and the door came ajar, opening inward. Freya pushed the portal the rest of the way open and ordered, "Get in there."

IT WAS A small room dominated by a short green metal table surrounded by six chairs that had lime-colored metal frames with dark avocado padding for seats and backrests. The walls, ceiling, and floor were all green, as was the window frame. The pane in the window was painted lime. The institutional chamber reminded Ronnie of jail.

"What the fuck are you doin' here, Ronnie Bottoms?" Freya said sharply. "And how the hell did you find me in the first place?"

"I know it's hard to believe, but I wasn't lookin' for you, Frey," Ronnie said. "It's like I told your man Alfred, I'm here to see Miss Peters."

"What happened to you?" Freya asked, not caring about or listening to what Ronnie had to say.

Her skin was dark like his, and her face pretty though its visage was petulant. She wore a loose-fitting coral-colored dress under a beige woman's sports jacket—both of which served to mute the power of her childbearing figure.

"What do you mean?" he asked.

"Your body look different an' them clothes," she said, "an' I don't remember you havin' no green eye."

"I got this infection when I was up at Rikers. The doctor at the infirmary told me that it wouldn't kill me or nuthin', but it could do that to your eyes. And I guess I lost some weight."

"And you look taller," she said with some uncertainty.

"Yeah. I grew some too."

"What you want with Miss Peters?"

She made love like that, changing the subject from one minute to the next, but Ronnie didn't mind back then or now.

"When I got out, I started thinkin' 'bout when I was in her class and how nice she was to me. It seems like everything good I remember comes from those two years I spent in the second grade. I feel like everything I know good I learned from her. She taught me about dinosaurs and myths and how the stars told stories."

Freya was frowning at her one-night lover from three and a half years before. "I ain't like I was no more," she said. "I'm a teacher's assistant, and I plan to get my degree."

"I cain't lie, Frey. I was gonna look you up too. But I'm happy you in school. If you don't wanna get together, I could see that. I mean the last time you seen me, I was just a thug."

"And now you got a green eye you different?"

Ronnie smiled and shook his head. "No, baby. That's just a color. I am different, but you don't have to believe it. No, ma'am. I know what I was and I know there ain't no talkin' gonna convince somebody otherwise."

"You really didn't come here to see me?" Freya asked.

Ronnie shook his head no.

"'Cause if the people here connect me up with a hoodlum like you, I'm bound to lose this job."

"I'll just tell 'em you knew my older sister, Tiffany. That way it's like a family thing and you know you cain't help who your family is."

"If I leave you here, you won't do nuthin' to get me in trouble?"

"Are you gonna go get Miss Peters?"

"I'll ask her if she wants to see you."

"Then I will sit in that green chair over there and wait. That's all."

"And you know Miss Peters for real?"

"Tell her that it's Ronnie Bottoms from her second-grade class, the one that she kept in from recess and lunch period every day."

TWENTY-SIX

ALONE IN THE green room, Ronnie relaxed. He had spent most of his life in detainment of one type or another; like when he was sent to the bedroom that he shared with his brother, Myron, when he was bad. Later he'd been sentenced to juvenile hall, jail, and even prison. When he went to school, he often had detention either in the vice principal's office or in a room presided over by the dour Mr. Gorsh.

The calm he was experiencing came from a sense of arrival. He left the rich girl's condo, defeated Fast Freddie, got around the security guard, and had finally reached the locked room where he was waiting with no food or water or any idea of what Freya was doing.

After a while he went to the opaque lime-colored window and tried to slide it open, but it was bolted and nailed shut.

When he turned back to the table, Used-to-be-Claude was sitting there shirtless and shoeless in a red suit. His legs were crossed comfortably and he smiled for Ronnie.

"I can't stay here too long," the husk of the dead wino said.

"Is any'a this real?" Ronnie asked as he took the seat next to the simulacrum.

Still smiling, Used-to-be-Claude said, "Even ideas and wishes have form and weight. It is impossible to have conception without a supplemental series of potential and actual realities. The problem starts when those realities are misperceived."

"You know I don't understand what you sayin', right?"

"You came here to visit your teacher from long ago," Used-to-be-Claude said. "Why?"

"I been thinkin' about her."

"You thought about her and now you are here."

"But maybe I ain't here," Ronnie reasoned. "Maybe you made all this up and then made me think it was true."

"Even if that were so," Used-to-be-Claude said patiently, "who's to say that some even greater power didn't cause me to fool you?"

"Why you in a hurry?" Ronnie said, already tired of the pointless debate.

"I cannot let the Laz find me here."

"I thought he couldn't see you."

"When I am close to you or Lorraine, I am rendered partially visible to him."

"What if you were with the both of us together?"

"If we were not within my earthly stronghold, I would shine like a nova star. The Laz is orbiting the globe, dipping down now and then into those souls that it might corrupt. It's looking for a host to defeat you with."

"Can you tell us where it's at?"

"I cannot see."

"But that's what made Cosmo so sad about breakin' that girl's heart?"

Used-to-be-Claude nodded and clasped his hands. "I do not wish to destroy this world, Ronnie Bottoms. You and Lorraine Fell must find the Laz and bring it to me. You must bind him and blind him and make him helpless. Then I will do what I must."

Used-to-be-Claude got to his feet and Ronnie stood also.

"You got it, brother" Ronnie said, extending a hand.

Instead of returning the gesture, Used-to-be-Claude hopped backwards almost to the olive wall, making sure to avoid contact.

"What?" Ronnie asked.

At that moment, the door to the green room came open, Used-to-be-Claude evaporated in a silent puff of multicolored mist, and for a moment Ronnie thought he saw the double of the red ring that had infected the lingering disease of Cosmo's perfidy.

Ronnie turned to the door to see a tallish white woman in a gray dress suit and yellow-rimmed glasses.

"Ronnie?" the woman said.

The hem of her dress was down below the knee and there was one big pocket on her left thigh. And though her hair had more gray to it, her face didn't look any different. This amazed the young man. It had to be at least seventeen years since he'd last seen her.

"Miss Peters?"

"How are you?" The teacher walked right up and put her arms around him.

Used-to-be-Claude out of mind, Ronnie remembered that Miss Peters would always hug him when they were alone during recess or lunch. She'd do that until he calmed down and then tell him stories or show him how to use art tools.

"Come sit," she said. "Come."

She took him by the arm and sat as he did.

She was holding his right hand with both of hers.

"How have you been?" she asked.

"All ovah the place really," he said, feeling the words flow easily, "in trouble a lot but I think that's mostly ovah now. I been in and outta jail and my mama died—"

"I'm so sorry to hear that. Your mother was a lovely woman."

"You knew my mama?"

"She would come by every Thursday afternoon and we'd talk about you."

"You mean me and Tiffany and Myron."

"Sometimes we'd talk about your brother and sister, but mostly it was just you."

"Really?"

Shona Peters had a heart-shaped face and a small mouth but thick lips. Her skin color was cream and her eyes doe brown.

"What happened to your eye?" she asked.

"I got an infection when I was in jail."

"But you're out of that now."

It was then that Ronnie recalled that he had an afternoon appointment with his parole officer that day.

"Yes, ma'am," he said.

"Why did you come here?" Miss Peters asked. "Do you need anything?"

"No. I got money and a place to live and all. I guess because I got time to think now, I was tryin' to remember what was good in my life. All I could think of was my mama and you. She really used to come here?"

"Every week she would. We talked about how hard it was for you to concentrate on any one thing for very long. She told me what a loving son you were, about how you made her morning tea at least three times a week."

"I remember that too. I also remember about the myths and the stars and how ants know each other by smell. You said that all bees was girl bees except when the queen needed to mate—"

Shona placed the palm of her right hand against the grown man's cheek and he began to weep. There was no sound or gasping, just a flow of tears for something both lost and found.

That was how Freya found them when she entered the green room twenty minutes later.

"You told me to tell you when it was eleven," she said to Miss Peters.

"Do you need me to stay?" Miss Peters asked Ronnie.

"I could sit here wit' you for a whole mont'," Ronnie replied, unashamed of his tears.

In his mind he likened the weeping to the living waterfall in the Silver Box's Central Park fortress. It also brought to mind the times when Mr. Charles Burns would hose down the sidewalk in front of the old 156th Street apartment that

Ronnie had lived in with his mother, brother, and sister. It felt good to see the dirt washed up from between the cracks and crevices and flushed into the gutter. Now and then Charles Burns would let Ronnie hold the hose, showing him how to make a spray by covering half its mouth with his tiny thumb. The pressure of the water tickled.

Miss Peters was looking at him, patient with his wandering mind as she had always been.

"But I got to go too," Ronnie said at last.

"Shall we stand up, then?" Miss Peters suggested.

That was how she got him ready when recess was over. He wanted her all to himself but when she said those words, he knew that he'd have to go back to his desk and wait for the other kids.

"Freya will see you to the exit," the elementary school teacher said at the green door.

"Miss Peters?"

"Yes, Ronnie?"

"I got a 'partment down on Fifth Avenue with a roommate. You wanna come down sometime and have dinner with us?"

"Let me see your arm," the teacher said.

Obediently Ronnie stuck out his left hand with the palm up. Shona Peters took out a blue ink pen from the big pocket in her dress and wrote a ten-digit number on his inner forearm.

"That's how you used to remind me about my home homework," he said in revelation. "You'd write it on my arm and when Mama asked me if I had studies and I said no, she'd tell me to ask my arm if that was true."

The teacher kissed his cheek and said, "Freya will take you."

As she was walking away, Ronnie wanted to yell something but he didn't think it was right.

"YOU REALLY GOT an apartment on Fifth Avenue?" Freya asked him on the granite front stairs of the school.

"Uh-huh." He was running his fingers lightly across the phone number on his written-upon arm.

"Are you gonna ask me ovah for some dinner?"

TWENTY-SEVEN

ONLY MINUTES AFTER she left Ronnie, Lorraine had made
her way to the pedestrian path that ran along the Hudson
River and went all the way up to the George Washington
Bridge. From there she headed inland and through a large
park she'd found.

She wasn't going very fast, just like a sprinter in a
hundred-meter race. For her this pace felt like an easy jog.
She speeded up when crossing at red lights or to avoid
collisions with slow-moving pedestrians or cars. The run
wasn't so fast or satisfying as it had been on the yellow dirt
path but it was enough to take the edge off the tension she
had been feeling in her thighs.

She came to a halt at a lonely bus stop where a young
bespectacled white man was sitting reading a hardback
book. An older black woman was seated on the other end
of the bench.

Lorraine stood over the young man and looked down

on him. He was thin and his shaggy brown hair had grown over his ears. He didn't notice the runner.

"Hi," she said.

He looked up, squinting from the bright sun behind her. "Hi."

"Can I sit with you?"

"Sure. It's a public bench."

She sat close enough that her left thigh was pressing up against his right. He made the motion of moving over, but he was already at the edge of the bench.

"What you reading?"

"One Hundred Years of Solitude."

"Critics called it magic realism, but García Márquez says that every word is true," she said. "I like it when God calls down for the beautiful young maiden to float up to heaven."

"You read it?"

"Could you help me?" she replied.

"Wha-what?"

"I need a boy to kiss me a little bit."

"Huh?"

"We could go over in that alley over there. That way if the bus comes, you could still make it."

The older black woman was staring as the newly met young couple walked into the deserted brick and concrete alley.

There was a black door a third of the way down the lane. It was set in a foot or so and Lorraine pushed him against it.

When she kissed him, it was with her entire body: shoulders and breasts, pelvis and thighs—not to mention her lips and tongue.

The young man—she found out later that his name was Alton—had never felt passion like this from a woman. His girlfriend of three years, Christine, didn't like kissing. She had read somewhere that there were always crumbs of food in peoples' mouths, and after that, kissing always felt dirty.

Lorraine enjoyed swabbing her tongue around and under his tongue and between his teeth and lips. She reveled in the little sighs and grunts of surprise and pleasure that came from him. When she put her hand down the front of his jeans, he froze.

"Calm down," she said. "Nobody can see."

She pushed his shoulder back with her left hand while with her right she moved up and down at an impossible rate while making sure not to hold the erection too tightly. She watched his face contort.

He tried to grope under her dress but she said, "No. I'm doing you," and he stopped.

When he started to make a gasping cry, she whispered, "The bus is coming. Do you want me to stop?"

"No, no, no, no," he said, each syllable punctuating a pulse of his orgasm.

Lorraine smiled and held tight to Alton's erection. His eyes opened wide, trying to see as much of this strange young woman as he could.

"Okay," she said. "You got to brace yourself, 'cause I'm gonna do it again."

A WHILE LATER they were sitting at the bus stop. The older black woman had taken the bus. Alton was holding the book and trying to think of something to say to the olive-skinned blond-haired girl with the multicolored eyes.

"If you want more than that," she said after a while, "you can come with me to another bench down from my parents' condo on the Upper East Side. If you wait while I'm up there arguing with them, I'll take you home afterwards and fuck your brains out."

Lorraine heard these words coming from her lips, knew that it was her on that bench next to the egghead commuter, but she didn't feel like herself. Her death and revivification had left her with what felt like an open heart—vulnerable to every passion and willing—no, compelled—to act on whatever it was she felt.

Before her encounter with Ronnie Bottoms and the Silver Box, Lorraine had made the time to read a book almost every day. If she did not have the time to read, she got nervous and sad. But after her death, she had no interest in the written word or thoughts that not did not lead to sensual expression.

"MISS LORRAINE!" NOVA Triphammer-Louise exclaimed at the front door of the Fell condo.

"Miss Nova," Lorraine replied as was their ritual.

"Girl, you look too skinny and what happened with your eyes?"

"I've actually gained weight," Loraine said as she walked into the vestibule and then down the long hallway toward the sitting room. "And I was sick. A doctor told me that this sometimes happens when people get certain infections."

"But you're okay now," the lifetime housekeeper said.

"Never been better or clearer or happier."

They had reached the large sitting room, which was replete with a white and blue marble bar, a picture window looking onto a terrace that hovered above the East River, original oils that were insured for ten million dollars, and a teak worktable that Lorraine, her parents, and her brother, Damian, worked at when she was young.

Mr. Patrick Fell was tall and dashing except for his pale complexion. He played tennis, golf, and rode horses in jumping competitions from Connecticut to Virginia. His blond hair was seeded now with gray but he looked forty rather than fifty. His usual smile was missing, but other than that he was as he had always been.

Mrs. Alora Teeman-Fell was also tall and slender. She played tennis doubles with her husband and ran three miles a day. She was a vegetarian except when her mother came from Columbus to visit, and aloof, though Lorraine was always sure of her love.

"We expected you sooner than this," Mr. Fell said to his daughter.

"I've been busy."

"Let's sit down," Mr. Fell said.

Obediently Alora went to a chair at the near end of the long table, lowering onto it with exceptional poise.

Lorraine had always felt awkward in the presence of her mother.

"I'd rather stand," Lorraine said. She was feeling the tension of this meeting in her legs.

"I said, sit down."

"No."

"This is my house, Lore."

"And this is my ass, Dad. I will remain standing."

"Lorraine!" Alora Teeman-Fell complained.

"No, Mom. No. I came here because I knew you'd be upset. I want to talk to you about it, but I will not be bullied."

"I'm not bullying you," her father said, holding up a finger that was both instructional and threatening.

"Then don't tell me when to sit like I'm some kind of fucking dog."

Lorraine was continually surprised by her own quick temper. She'd almost killed Lance. She *had* killed Ma Lin. All her manners and good upbringing seemed to have drained away with death. She had jettisoned the restrictive limitations like a too-tight corset or four-inch high heels and was now ready to run. This thought brought a smile to her face while her mother fretted and Mr. Fell scowled.

"I will not have that kind of language in my house, young lady," he said.

"You called Uncle Bernie a fucking horse's ass in this very room," she replied. "It was Thanksgiving dinner, and Mom laughed."

"He's not really your uncle," Alora objected.

Lorraine smiled and then grinned.

"Lance Figueroa called to tell us that you're living with

that black thug," her father said, "in the condo that I put the down payment on."

"You want me to move?"

"I want him out of there. I want you to come to your senses."

"Ronnie saved my life," she said. "He's homeless and he's trying to do what's right. He sleeps on the couch and even if he were in my bed, you have no right to tell me what to do in my own home."

"I can stop paying the mortgage."

"That's your choice," Lorraine agreed. "Is that all you want from me?"

"Lore," her father pleaded. "I'm your father."

"You are," she said, "but what you don't understand is that I am no longer your little girl." This was it. This was why she had come, why she ran for miles and then dominated bookish Alton Brown.

"The child you knew is gone from this body," she continued. "She's dropping out of Columbia. She's not sitting when you tell her to. If you stop paying the mortgage, she doesn't care one whit. It would be best for you and Mom to think that I had died when I went missing and that the girl you knew is gone from the world."

"But, honey," Alora said. "We love you."

The words sounded uncomfortable in the socialite's mouth, but Lorraine believed them anyway.

"I know, Mom," she said. "I know, but the Lorraine you love is a memory now. She doesn't fit into the world we lived in. You still have Papa and Damian. You still have all those times that we spent. If you want to get to know me and understand how much I've changed, I'll make sure that you always have my address and number."

Alora burst into loud crying, the tears literally jumping from her eyes.

Lorraine had never seen her mother cry before; neither had her husband or Nova, who came running from some hidden nook to comfort her employer. Patrick Fell also hurried to his wife's side.

From what seemed like a great distance, Lorraine watched the family unit so torn by her death. Alora wailed while the black servant and the white aristocrat tried to restrain her flailing arms.

The dead daughter quietly exited the room and the home she had known so well. Downstairs, in the concrete turnabout that looked over the East River, she found Alton Brown with *One Hundred Years of Solitude* unopened on his lap.

"You waited," she said.

"I never met anybody like you before."

"I know. You want to go fuck now?"

He stood up quickly and Lorraine grinned.

TWENTY-EIGHT

"You don't talk very much, huh?" Alton Brown asked Lorraine Fell on the long walk from her parents' Upper East Side condo down to her place on Fifth.

"I used to," she said, consciously slowing her pace. Lorraine's legs wanted to run but she needed company after bringing so much pain into her parents' lives. "Though I never said anything."

"You must have told people about how you felt and what you liked and didn't," Alton argued. "That's something."

"You ever had some smart kid in one of your a graduate seminars who would go home and in one night read the entire *Grundrisse* or *Moby-Dick*? And then at the next class meeting they would be able to recall long quotes along with the page numbers for all the salient moments that had to do with that day's lecture?"

"What's the *Grundrisse*?"

"*Capital* was the first part of six separate sections Marx conceived on political economy," Lorraine said, feeling like the smart-assed student she'd been before she died. "Though unfinished, the *Grundrisse* was all the other five."

"Yeah," Alton said. "Ben Smithy."

"Who's that?"

"The guy you're talking about," Alton said. "The guy who seemed to know everything about what you were studying in class. He would also know how all the ideas came together and proved, or didn't, whatever anybody said about it. We all hated him because he acted like he was so far ahead of us."

"I was Ben Smithy," Lorraine said. "I read books fast as a goddamn laser copy machine. I knew three different versions of Whitman's *Leaves of Grass* by heart, and I learned German so I could study everything from Kant to the Frankfurt School in the original texts. I ran a marathon, had the most beautiful boyfriend you could imagine, my parents are rich, and I believed that all that stuff made me a superior kind of person. But even then I never compared myself to anyone else, because I knew that hubris would make me seem like I wasn't absolutely perfect."

"Wow," Alton said.

Lorraine stopped walking and Alton did too.

She balled her fists and wondered why the rage had grown so suddenly in her heart.

"But you know what?" she asked.

"What?"

"I couldn't write one poem. I didn't have a single original thought in my head. I was a high-functioning fool who never, not even one time, took a chance on anything I might fail at."

"Like what?"

"Like asking some boy on a bus stop bench if he wanted to kiss me. Like taking a metal shop class in high school."

"Why not?"

Lorraine turned and started walking again. Alton had to scurry after her because she had picked up the pace.

"Because I thought that if I stayed perfect in everything that I'd never die or get old."

"That's kinda crazy, isn't it?"

Lorraine stopped again, grabbed Alton's shirt with both hands, and, using her body as a counterweight, swung him around until he was teetering on the edge of the curb. Cars were careening by just a foot or two away, but the young man didn't try to get away from the hold. He just stared at the rage in Lorraine's face.

Lorraine saw in his gaze a thirst for something, maybe knowledge; for the kind of awareness that was physical and real.

She pulled him back on the sidewalk and said, "I live with this guy."

"At the place we're going?"

"Yeah."

"Won't he mind if you, you bring me there?"

"No."

"Is he your lover?"

"The way I felt when I did everything perfectly," Lorraine said instead of answering the question, "was that if I died by mistake, I could actually come up out of the grave and make God give me my life back."

Fear and wonderment took over the geography of Alton's face. Lorraine felt like laughing at him but she didn't.

"Ronnie's not my lover," she said. "Sometimes I don't even like him."

"So . . . so why do you live together?"

"Sometimes," she said, "most of the time there's no reason for a thing to be. People like me and Ben Smithy like to pretend that there's a reason behind everything but we can't write one word from our hearts. All we do, all I ever did was walk down the path laid out in front of me and then brag about how I knew how to put one foot after the other."

She started walking again; this time slowly, looking inward.

"You're really deep," Alton said after they had gone a block or so in silence.

Three minutes later Lorraine said, "I used to be. But now I know that all the books I read were just exercises when I needed something deeper, real . . . absolute."

"Like what?"

"Death."

"How do you mean that?"

"I mean that Death came up and grabbed me by my throat. He choked me until I was either unconscious or dead. And there I was—in a limbo that I had no idea existed—and I knew all of a sudden that I had wasted all the minutes of my life leading up to the last moment.

"Can you understand how that feels?"

Alton, still looking for something, had no words but simply shook his head no.

"I want you to fuck me, Alton."

"Right here?"

The question and the fear that framed it made Lorraine laugh.

"No," she said. "Don't worry. I'm not crazy. It's just that I live by a different set of rules now."

"I'd like to know what they are," he said.

"Me too."

TWENTY-NINE

EARLIER THAT DAY, at 2:27 in the afternoon, Ronnie Bottoms arrived at the third-floor office of Florence Steinmetz—his court-appointed parole officer.

The third floor was only Department of Corrections business. The front desk was tenanted by a burly, florid-faced man dressed in a green corrections department uniform that was a size too small.

"Ronnie Bottoms for Miss Steinmetz," Ronnie said. "It's a two thirty appointment."

The doubtful officer looked down on his daily admittance sheet, tracing it with a cigarette-stained thumb. "I don't see you."

"Could you call her office?" Ronnie asked. "She is my PO and I need to know when to come back."

The big man—his nameplate read TRUMAN—sighed heavily and then picked up his phone. He hit three digits and grunted.

"Yeah," he said, "Truman here. I got a—What was your name again?"

"Ronnie Bottoms."

"—a Ronnie Bottoms thinks he's got a two thirty with Flo." Truman waited a moment and then said, "Okay. You got it." He cradled the phone and looked up at Ronnie. "Have a seat, Ronnie. Somebody will be with you in a moment."

The sentry nodded at a pine chair against the wall next to the door Ronnie was buzzed in through. The would-have-been young killer thought that, even though it was probably locked, he could break that door down if he wanted . . . and he did want to. There was something in Truman's tone that told him he was in trouble. It was a timbre he'd often heard in the voices of policemen, school-teachers, and various criminals, which warned of reprisal for some sin or oversight. It was the same sound Fast Fred-die had had in his voice when he sought to dominate Ronnie in the park.

He wanted to run, but instead Ronnie sat in the chair and waited.

In the large room beyond Truman's chair, people were moving about, and muted voices could be heard. Clicks and buzzes, now and then a recognizable word, and ringing phones sounded at odd moments, and there was a smell of disinfectant in the air. This was another institutional space, like the green room at his old elementary school or his twelve-man cell at Rikers. Rooms like this had been his home for many, many years and though he didn't like it, he was familiar with the impersonal attitudes and the smell of sterilizing chemicals.

While he was having this minor revelation, a door to Ronnie's right flung open. Three more uniforms came in at double-step.

"On your feet, Bottoms," Officer Truman said.

This too, Ronnie thought, was home.

They forced his arms behind his back and handcuffed him even though he offered no resistance.

They flanked him from every side and pushed him into the larger office space, where correction department employees worked at about a dozen desks, keeping the system of parole and reincarceration working.

No one looked up at the prisoner except for a redheaded young woman who seemed surprised. Ronnie gave the woman a wan smile and shrugged.

"Move it!" one of the uniforms said, and Ronnie was shoved through a doorway into an office that he'd been in only one time before.

The woman behind the desk was broad and square from her diaphragm to her shoulders, and she had a blocky face. Her brunet hair was streaked with gray and she wore a jacket that was also brown and gray. Her eyes were an unexpected festive blue. She was fifty or maybe sixty and had not had a good day for some time.

Seeing this woman, another revelation dawned upon Ronnie: Prison guards and administrators spent most of their waking hours in the same spaces that he did. They were all prisoners together.

"Ronnie Bottoms, ma'am," one of the guards said.

Florence Steinmetz's face was hard, unforgiving . . . at first. But as she looked at Ronnie, a question entered through the flesh around her eyes.

"What happened to you?" she asked.

Before he could process the question, someone from behind yanked up on his arm and said, "Answer the woman."

"Stop that, Martins," Steinmetz said. "Release Mr. Bottoms and let him sit."

"But, ma'am—"

"Do as I say. And when you've done that, you can wait outside the door."

"But we can leave it open, right?"

She nodded. The guards unlocked his chains, and Ronnie was allowed to sit in the PO's visitor's chair.

He sat, feeling distant from those environs.

"What happened to you?" Florence Steinmetz asked again.

"I don't know what you mean, Ms. Steinmetz."

"You look like you lost fifty pounds, and what's going on with those eyes?"

"Oh, yeah. It's kinda hard to explain, but I got, I got sick. It was like I couldn't move or nuthin' like that. It went on for a long time, and then, then it just went away. But how come you're arrestin' me?"

"You were supposed to report here last week."

"Oh." He had lost track of time. Somehow between the Silver Box, Ma Lin, the construction worker, and the Laz, a week had passed. "I didn't realize that. I thought this was supposed to be my second visit."

"That's a pretty lame excuse, wouldn't you say?"

"More like paralyzed."

Steinmetz allowed a quick smile to escape her lips, and Ronnie realized that he might not have to go to jail, that maybe he would make his dinner date with Freya Levering.

"You were really sick?"

"I swear I thought I was gonna die."

"I suppose you haven't found a job yet?" Steinmetz said.

"No, ma'am."

"There's a new barbecue place on Eighth up near Pennsylvania Station," she said. "Farnham's Pork House. They said that they'd take one of my guys. Would you like that job?"

"Sure . . . I mean, yeah."

"Come over here and let me see that eye."

Ronnie went around the desk and allowed his PO to spread open his eyelids with her thumb and forefinger.

"It's not a contact."

"No, ma'am. It's been like that since after I got sick." This was only technically a lie.

"Did you go to a doctor?"

"When I was sick, I couldn't get up, and when I was better it didn't seem like I needed to."

ON THE WALK up to Lorraine's condo, Ronnie contemplated his luck.

In the two and a half decades leading up to the Silver Box, his entire lifetime, Ronnie could always rely on his luck—his bad luck. Whatever could go wrong did go wrong. "If he was climbing out the window of an apartment he'd just robbed, there was a cop coming around the corner of the alley below. If he loved somebody, they either died like his mother or betrayed him like most girlfriends he'd had. If he beat somebody in a fight, they had bigger brothers. If he lost a battle, the victor always kicked him when he was down."

But now his luck had changed.

The Silver Box and Lorraine had not only saved his soul from a murder rap but also given him a smidgen of good luck. He didn't break down the door to get away from Officer Truman and so left open the possibility that Ms. Steinmetz might show him leniency. He got a job at the barbecue place with just a phone call. Now he was going to meet a woman who had a job, an education, and a rolling gait that made him smile.

He had eight hundred dollars in his pocket and no desire to spend it. He hadn't been high for many days, and so the urine test at the PO's office wouldn't get him into trouble.

Ronnie laughed out loud, and people on the street quickened their steps to avoid his madness.

THIRTY

"*WHO IS THIS* Lorraine Fell?" Freya asked Ronnie as they rode the elevator up to the twenty-third floor of the fancy condo building. She had been waiting for him outside when he got back from the parole meeting.

The doorman, Travis Jeffers, challenged the couple, saying that Ms. Fell had said that only Ronnie was allowed access to the condo. But when Ronnie asked to speak to the building manager, Jeffers stood down and allowed the two to pass.

"She's my roommate," Ronnie said in the elevator.

"Girlfriend?"

"No. You think I'm stupid enough to take another woman to my girlfriend's apartment?"

Freya looked doubtfully at Ronnie, and he laughed out loud.

———

"*THIS IS NICE,*" Freya said.

They were sitting on a blue sofa and looking out on the evening lights of Manhattan, eating pizza and drinking red wine from Lorraine's built-in wine cooler.

The teacher's assistant was surprised that Ronnie had only kissed her a few times. And he'd had only one slice of the plain cheese pie. His reserve was somehow kindling her passions.

"Yeah," he said.

"How come she let you live here?"

"I found her almost dead and helped her get better. Now she needs me around because she's scared of her nightmares." Ronnie had to lie, but he wanted to lay the truth in with fabrication.

"And she not your girlfriend?"

"Not at all."

"An' you don't even sleep with her?"

"I have held her at night after she had bad dreams, but I'm not attracted to her in a sex way."

"What kinda infection you say you had?" Freya asked.

"Bad."

"It musta been. There you are cryin' with Miss Peters and here I am in a room alone with you and you ain't pullin' on my clothes. Now you say a woman bring you to her bed an' you don't feel in the sex way. Damn."

Ronnie stood up then and lifted the small rounded woman like she was a doll. He wrapped his arms under her rump and kissed her—long and slow. The weightlessness and unexpected strength frightened her at first, but then the kiss took over her senses.

The minutes passed and Ronnie felt good kissing the teaching assistant's lips and eyes, cheeks and neck. She actually moaned from the tender osculations. Ronnie was surprised and happy that he could make a woman feel this way with just a kiss.

"Baby," she said.

"What?" he slurred while pressing the tip of his tongue lightly into her ear.

"Ain't your arms gettin' tired?"

"I could hold you and kiss you like this all night long."

"But don't you wanna lie down on the couch?"

"Is that you want?"

"Uh-huh."

He tipped forward slightly, causing her to lean back from him. Staring into her gaze, he was motionless for a moment.

"Please put me down and lie there with me," she said, almost breathless.

Shifting with no apparent exertion, he laid her down on the wide blue sofa. He kissed her and she groaned impatiently. He smiled at her and touched her face.

The front door came open just then.

"Hi, Ronnie."

Freya sat up and saw a slender young white woman with a tan and dirty blond hair followed by an even skinnier white youth coming after her like a dog that just can't get enough of its master.

"Lore," Ronnie said, his voice deep and husky.

"Who's this?"

"Freya. She gonna stay here wit' me tonight."

"This is Alton Brown. Say hello, Alton."

"Hey."

"You're welcome in my home, Freya," Lorraine said. "I'm going to turn my study into Ronnie's bedroom before too long. That way you two can have some privacy."

"Um . . . Thank you," the teacher's assistant said. "It's nice to meet you."

Lorraine took Alton by the hand and walked him into her bedroom.

After a minute or two, the young white couple were making enough noise to be heard beyond the door.

But Ronnie and Freya didn't hear them.

"RONNIE!"

Freya was the first to awaken. Sinewy and naked, Lorraine Fell—her eyes unfocused, her hands shaking—was standing over her.

Ronnie grunted and sat up.

Lorraine yelped from some inner fear and Ronnie took her by the hand.

"It's okay, Lore," he said. "It's all right."

Groaning he stood up, cradled and lifted his landlady, victim, best friend, and fellow conspirator. She fell instantly asleep in his arms.

The big man then lowered next to Freya with the sleeping Lorraine on his other side, her head on his lap.

"What's wrong with her?" Freya asked. She sat up and wrapped Ronnie's shirt around her shoulders.

"It's the nightmares I told you about. She get 'em and I

have to be there or she'll never fall asleep. It's how she, um, she bonded with me after I saved her."

"And she always come out naked like that?"

"Uh-huh, mostly."

"An' you don't try an' take advantage?"

Ronnie stared again at his lover. She was beautiful and vulnerable but still strong. While appreciating her, he could feel Lorraine's spirit self—the part of her that was cut free for a time after he killed her—floating somewhere in the atmosphere above her. If he had slept with her, they would have begun their nighttime crawl after the spirit spoor of the Laz escapee. But because he was still awake, she just floated like a cloud riding on an updraft from a deep subterranean cavern.

"Ronnie?" It was Freya.

"Yeah?"

"I asked didn't you ever take advantage of her?"

He smiled again. "Ain't nobody gonna take advantage'a this girl here. But if you askin' if I fucked her, the answer is no. I'm her friend and that's just like a locked door for me."

"Since when?"

"I'm a changed man, Frey. You could see that, right?"

"I guess."

"I ain't runnin' after shit no mo'. Damn . . . enough shit done come after me all these years. All I want is to settle down, maybe learn how to read bettah, and make something right here while I got the time."

Freya reached out to touch Ronnie's face.

"What happened to you?" she asked.

"It sounds crazy."

"Crazier than a niggah like you turnin' away when a fine girl drop her draws in front'a you?"

"It's like one day," Ronnie said, "I gave birth to myself."

"Like a woman?"

"Yeah. Or maybe it was like the snakes Miss Peters used to talk about—the ones that pop right outta their skin an' come out like new."

"You remembah that?" Freya asked.

"I remembah everything she said."

"You are like new," Freya agreed.

"That's right," Ronnie said, and then he held out his hand for her to take. "We all in different dreams, everybody in the whole world. But there's a place where those dreams come together and, and, and when that happens it's just so beautiful that it hurts."

"And that's how it is with you and this girl?"

"Yeah. She all rich and white and shit, and here I am straight outta the hood. But we come together and there's like a, a mission or a calling that we both have to do."

Freya squeezed his hand and said, "You might scare me more now than you did when you was a thug, Ronnie Bottoms."

"What's going on out here?" Alton Brown asked. He was clad only in a pair of pale blue boxer shorts.

"Lore had a bad dream and needed to lay her head down," Ronnie said.

"Why did she have to come out here?"

Ronnie gave the half-true explanation he'd concocted, and Alton sat down on the solid block of a coffee table.

"You guys are real close, huh?" Alton asked.

"In a funny kinda way. I mean, I don't know hardly nuthin' about her, nor she me. But we connected like, like two different kindsa rocks rolled up on a beach." Ronnie was remembering one of the many things he'd learned and heard from Ms. Peters.

"But you're not her boyfriend?"

"Naw, man. That's you."

"How long have you known each other?" Alton asked.

"Me and Lore or me and Frey?"

"Lorraine."

" 'Bout a mont'. We used to watch the same cartoons when we was kids. Once we knew we did that, we found that we had other things the same."

"I just met Lorraine today," the skinny intellectual said. "I guess you could say that she swept me off my feet."

"That's Lorraine, all right," Ronnie said. "She like the goddamned wind."

"What do you do?" Freya asked Alton.

"I study literature at CCNY."

"Books?" she asked.

"Mostly, but now they have all this what they call theory. Trying to make art into a science kind of."

"I've heard a dude once said that in the beginning there was only science," Ronnie said, "that machines were the first true intelligence and that flesh and blood life came after."

"How could that be?" Freya said in a superior tone.

"Right now computers think faster than men," Ronnie said, defending an uncertain turf. "They learn all kindsa shit. If you can imagine, then you could make it real. Matter'a fact if you imgine sumpin', it is real, at least in your mind."

"Do you go to college?" Alton asked his lover's roommate.

Freya laughed.

"Hey, man, why don't you grab a sofa an' get some sleep," Ronnie offered. "You know Lore ain't gonna wake up till mornin'."

"Maybe you should put her down next to me."

"No, brother. If I let her go, she'll just get all crazy again. Don't worry, though—we'll be right here across from you."

And so Alton lay down on the opposite blue sofa while Ronnie sat upright with Freya's head on his shoulder and Lorraine's head in his lap. He closed his eyes, conjured up his mother's heartbeat, and fell asleep feeling that she was, once again, alive.

THIRTY-ONE

"COME ON, GUYS, wake up," Lorraine Fell was saying.

She had on a coral pink dress that shimmered a bit. It was low cut with the hem at her knee. She'd done her long blond hair into two pigtails, one either side of her head. This made her look much younger.

When Ronnie opened his eyes and saw her, he smiled, happy to be alive at that moment, in that room.

Freya sat up, rubbing a kink in her neck, and Alton yawned, looking around bleary eyed. The lit student had a confused expression, as if he was trying to remember where he was and who he was with.

"What time is it?" Freya asked.

"Almost eight," Lorraine said.

"I'm gonna be late," the teacher's assistant whined. "I don't even have time to go home and change my clothes."

"You can take something from my closet," Lorraine offered. "I got all kinds of dresses and stuff. Then I'll get the doorman to call a car to take you to work."

"I don't have money for no car," Freya complained.

"They'll just put it on the unit bill."

"Really?"

"Sure. Come on, let me show you what I've got."

The young women went into the bedroom, and Ronnie pulled up his pants.

"This is all kind of crazy," Alton said.

"That might be," the ex-thug agreed, "but crazy is better than bad, and bad ain't the worst it could get."

"What do you mean?"

"Gettin' shot, stabbed and left for dead, or hunted down by both the cops and gangbangers," Ronnie enumerated. "I been on the wrong end of every one'a those situations. So wakin' up in a high-rise penthouse might be strange, but at least it ain't gonna kill me."

"I have a girlfriend," Alton replied.

"Now you got two."

"I don't think Christine would understand me spending the night with Lorraine."

"Okay. Now imagine Christine gettin' all mad an' comin' after you with a loaded pistol in her hand."

"She'd never do that."

"You see?" Ronnie said. "Things is bettah already."

FARNHAM'S PORK HOUSE was on Eighth Avenue just a little bit south of Penn Station. Ronnie's appointment was at 10 A.M., but he was there by 9:30.

He, Alton, and Freya, all accompanied by Lorraine, left the Van Dyne at the same time. The women had formed a temporary bond while Alton kept reaching out to touch Lorraine's arm or hand. It was as if he couldn't believe what had happened, what he had done.

"We should all meet tonight at Le Grand Chambre for dinner at nine," Lorraine said on the curb before Freya got into her car, wearing a light green dress made from raw silk that had been loose on Lorraine but fit Freya just right.

"Is it expensive?" Freya asked about the restaurant.

"I'm using my father's credit card, so as far as we're concerned, it's free," Lorraine replied. And then to Ronnie, "You and I should probably go to Used-to-be-Claude's little nest at six."

"Yeah," Ronnie agreed.

"CAN I GET something for you?" a café au lait–colored young woman said at the counter of the barbecue joint.

"My name is Bottoms. My parole officer, Miss Steinmetz, said that you guys had a job opening here."

"Parole officer?" the young woman said. Her name tag read NANCY. She had a buttery complexion and eyes that hovered between yellow and green, like fancy agate marbles.

"Yeah," Ronnie admitted. "I'm what they call on the temporary for two years, and I need a job or they'll throw me back in prison."

"Oh."

Seeing the concern on Nancy's face, Ronnie remembered that he was in a world where being an ex-con was not acceptable, like having your fly down or letting loose a ripe fart on crowded subway car.

"My parole officer, Florence Steinmetz, said that I had an appointment for a job interview here," Ronnie said, trying to make up for what he'd already said wrong.

"Oh," Nancy said again. "I mean, I'll go get Roger."

She turned away from the counter and went behind a shelf into an industrial kitchen where there were three or four people working.

Ronnie appreciated standing there in what was for him the early morning, without a hangover, and free.

"Anybody here?" someone said from behind.

It was a thirty-something white man in a dark blue uniform that was sturdily designed for labor not service.

"She went to get Roger," Ronnie said.

"Can't work for herself?"

"I'm askin' for a job, and Roger's the man to see."

"Then she should have sent somebody else to cover the counter," the black-haired white man said.

Ronnie could hear the anger in his voice. At any previous time, he would have started a fight with him even though now he couldn't conjure up a justification for the dead emotion.

"Can I help you?" another man's voice asked.

Ronnie turned back to the counter, seeing that Nancy and a short, wiry black man had come out from somewhere beyond the kitchen.

"I can take your order, sir," Nancy said to the angry white customer.

"It's about time you got your ass out here."

"Excuse me, sir," the manager, whom Ronnie figured to be about forty, said, "but I will not have my employees addressed with that kind of language."

"What?"

"This is a place of business, and I expect civility from my employees and my customers."

Ronnie liked this man, very much.

"If that's your attitude," the white workman said, "then you don't want my business."

"No, sir, I don't."

"You know I ought to climb over that counter and—," the workman got out.

"Excuse me," Ronnie said in a tone of voice that felt new to him, "but you should be goin' now."

There was something familiar in the sound of Ronnie's words to the workman, who had the name HOWARD stitched in red over his left breast pocket. Howard jerked backwards, turned, and walked out of the barbecue restaurant without uttering another word.

"I didn't need you to do that," the black man said.

"I wasn't doin' nuthin'," Ronnie responded. "He was about to lose his temper and there was no need for that. I mean, we just talkin' 'bout some babyback ribs and French fries, right?"

The manager's dark face broke into a smile. He pushed against his kinky salt-and-pepper hair with the three longest fingers of his left hand.

"My name's Roger Merryman," he said.

"Ronnie Bottoms. Miss Steinmetz send me down from the parole office."

"Come on in through the side door, Ronnie," Merryman offered.

"WHAT WERE YOU in for?" Roger Merryman asked Ronnie Bottoms in his storeroom-office at the back of fast-
food restaurant.

"They called it armed robbery, but I didn't use a weapon,"
Ronnie said. He was thinking about Lorraine; about how
he felt that something was missing when they were apart
for too long. "I mean it was more like assault and robbery,
but they don't have that in the sentencing book."

"So you'd just kick somebody's ass and then take their
wallet?" Roger was slight and dark with sharp features
and piercing brown eyes with topaz highlights.

"That's all ovah, man. I ain't like that no mo'."

"No?"

"Uh-uh."

"Why should I believe that?"

"Because before, if I was mad at a man like that dude
out front, I would'a hurt him."

"That's what you would have done if he wanted to start
a fight when you told him to leave?"

"No. Not no mo'."

"Then what would you have done?"

"I'da just grabbed him around the chest and carried
him out to the sidewalk. Aftah that he wouldn't even want
no trouble."

"Come on with me," Roger replied as if this were a response to Ronnie's claim.

ON THE *TWELVE-BY-TWENTY-SQUARE-FOOT* apron of concrete behind the restaurant, there were six big smokers made from black metal canisters set on their sides on sawhorse wooden frames.

Roger took a trash can the size of one of those smokers and put the nozzle of a water hose in it.

"This here is my meat kitchen," Roger said as he turned on the water at full force. "One each for chicken, sausages, pork ribs, beef ribs, brisket, and one for steaks and chops. These cans are something like you."

"Like me how?"

"They illegal. I'm not supposed to be smokin' meat outside like this. It breaks the health law."

"You pay off the cops and the health inspector?"

Roger smiled, and Ronnie wondered what made the little businessman agree to consider an ex-con for whatever position he had open.

"I used to be an armed robber," Roger said as if Ronnie had put his question into words. "But I learned how to read when I was in and made up my mind to go straight. Now I get here at four o'clock eve'ry mornin' and put a hundred pounds of meat in each can. I fire 'em up over coals and hickory chips. As we sell it off, I move the cooked meat to the right and add raw to the left. I put my father's special marinade over it all one after the other, then wait fifteen minutes and do it again. That's the job I want you for."

"I got to be here at four?"

"Naw. I'll come in then and start it all off. You come in at nine and work till six."

"Okay." Ronnie's entire body undulated with the agreement. He liked the idea of a job where he had all the skills he needed from the start.

"But there's one thing first," Roger, the diminutive ex-con manager said.

"What's that?"

"Turn off that water hose."

The water was brimming over the top of the big can.

Ronnie turned off the water and wondered if this were somehow the test.

"A gallon of water weighs eight point three five pounds," Roger said.

"If you say so."

"This can holds just about eighty gallons."

"Uh-huh."

"Pick it up by the handles and lift it as high as you can."

Ronnie squatted down in front of the can, got the heel of a palm under each handle; then he stood, thrusting up his arms as he did so. When his arms were fully extended and the water can was at the limit of his reach, he said, "Like this?"

Instead of answering, Roger watched Ronnie as the seconds ticked by. After a minute, the restaurateur said, "You can put it down now."

Ronnie slowly lowered the can, setting it on the concrete floor with barely a sound.

"You really coulda just put that white dude under your

arm and carried him out the door," Roger said behind a sly smile.

"Uh-huh. I could barbecue this meat too. You just need to show me when it's cooked enough to move ovah and then cooked so much that I have to take in the kitchen."

THIRTY-TWO

WHILE RONNIE WORKED the unlicensed smokers at the back of Farnham's Pork House, and the Silver Box's infinite circuits pondered the question of how it could have, if only for a micron of a nanosecond, lost concentration on its self-generated prime directive; while Freya Levering was herding a group of third-graders from the recess yard to their classroom, wondering at how the brutal Ronnie Bottoms had learned to kiss so softly and passionately; while the complex molecules that composed one ten-millionth of the Laz Inglo's soul darted through the stratosphere, *listening* for just the right vessel for its resurrection—while all of this transpired, Lorraine Fell was running.

She ran down Forty-second Street from Fifth Avenue to the West Side Highway. From there she kept a furious pace all the way up to the Henry Hudson Bridge, turned right, crossed the city, and was soon headed south all the way down to Wall Street and then back up again.

While running, she found that her sight was so intently focused that she could almost see the insides of things and people, intentions and history. Children's eyes spoke of the mammalian chronicle. Ancient buildings deconstructed, showing their foundations and bony girders under her scrutiny. The waters rose and laughed beside her, hinting at a kind of life that was unsuspected by her kind; by men and women who believed so profoundly in biological ascendance that they could not see the awareness of matter; that *things* were more complex than human consciousness, that the sun beating down on her head was aware of its power and of the limitations of all things, beings, and even machines.

Now and then Lorraine would stop, not because she was tired but to see the connection between her motion and her sight. When she was still, her knowledge became like memory, almost static. The waters receded into simple flowing. The sun shone but did not holler and brag. Children's eyes were inquisitive but no longer revealed bits and pieces of the long thread of material evolution that most scientists had mistaken for the only form of life.

When she started running again, a more complex comprehension dawned once more within her. It was as if this knowledge were separate from her or, more correctly, she was merely a small part of a greater awareness that could only be obtained by motion.

She made the circuit of Manhattan six times before the jitters in her bones were sated. Her body thrummed and her mind contained thoughts that were as vast as the terrain she traveled. By the time she got back to her condo, she was grinning like child at play.

When she came into the apartment, she heard sounds from the kitchen.

"Ronnie?"

"No, baby, it's me," Nova Triphammer-Louise said.

The mid-height, bottom-heavy, dark-skinned woman came from the kitchen, smiling with her perfect, slightly dulled teeth. Nova's face was round and handsome, her age somewhere past retirement.

Seeing the family servant, Lorraine felt a little like her old self again. She remembered the nights she would lie in bed, worrying about infinity, and Nova Louise would come sit beside her on the bed and they would sing hymns the old black woman knew by heart.

Nova wore black stretch pants and a peacock blue T-shirt. Her shoes were black fabric with white rubber soles.

"What are you doing here, Nova?"

"Cleanin' like I do every week. You et up all your cereal and milk. They're bein' delivered."

"How's Mom?"

"When she wouldn't stop cryin' after two days, your father called a woman doctor and she put her in a sanatorium up in Riverdale."

"Oh." In her mind, Lorraine realized she had turned away so completely from her family that they could have died and she might not have ever known. She, who was once a member of something, was now a lone soldier on foreign turf. She had, she felt, lost the world she'd belonged to and could not call up the desire in her heart to get it back.

She had few real feelings left for her past life, but the emptiness of this loss caused a kind of bereavement in her breast. She brought up a hand to place over the metaphorical wound.

Nova threw tan shammy cloth down on a blue sofa and went to take Lorraine in her arms. The young woman resisted at first but then surrendered to the embrace.

"What's wrong, baby?" Nova asked, her face in the profusion of damp blond hair.

"You remember when we used to sing 'Onward, Christian Soldiers'?"

"Of course I do," Nova whispered. "You used to always say 'leading off for more' instead of 'war.'"

They giggled together.

"That's kind of where I'm at."

"God will see you through."

"But he's too big, Novie, and I'm too small."

RONNIE RETURNED FROM his parolee job a few hours later, after Nova had gone. He found Lorraine sitting in the deep ledge at the window, looking out on Fifth Avenue.

"You smell like smoke," she said when he climbed in next to her.

"It's like bein' in a furnace all day long. But you know, I kinda like it. My boss keep a six-hundred-pound can'a water back there, and every now and then he bring some random dude back to see how I could lift it up."

Lorraine took Ronnie's hand and held it tight. "I've seen things that I can't understand, but I know them," she said.

"It's like you're a little kid on a merry-go-round," he intuited from that touch. "You're goin' and faster and faster and might fall off any minute, but you don't even care."

"You know that?"

"What can you tell about me?"

"That we need to find your family," she whispered, "and we have to trap Inglo so the Silver Box doesn't destroy the world."

"What else?"

"That we kind of like traded places," Lorraine said. "That my prison is your treasure and your anger was somehow hidden in my heart."

"Let's get dressed and go down to the park before we meet our dates," Ronnie told Lorraine, and she kissed his knuckle before traipsing off to her bedroom.

USED-TO-BE-CLAUDE AND MA LIN were waiting for them that early evening. The space inside the crevice of tall boulders was now as wide as six football fields. The stone table was a little larger and the living waterfall cascaded in the distance.

Ma Lin was standing with his hands behind his back in military fashion while UTB-Claude sat at the edge of the table in his black suit, now wearing a red shirt but still with no shoes or socks.

"Why don't you wear shoes, Claude?" Ronnie asked, feeling closer to the wino than to the ex-military cop.

"Because I don't need them."

"You don't need pants neither, but you wearin' 'em."

"Covering the loins is an older practice than sheathing the foot."

"We must hurry," Ma Lin said.

"Why?" Lorraine asked.

"Because we must."

"Are you the Silver Box?" she replied.

"I speak for it."

"But are you it?"

"No."

"Then don't order us around."

Ma Lin's eyes tightened, and his removed demeanor took on an intense focus. Ronnie wondered if his hands would once again become a bludgeon and a bayonet. But the ex-MP, ex–Inglo slave, the ex–human being turned abruptly and stalked off toward the distant waterfall that Ronnie knew was laughing at them.

"Lin's an experiment," UTB-Claude said. "Silver Box is everything, but that doesn't mean that it is just one being. It allows its separate units to have some autonomy. Even I'm a little different. I mean the man I'm based on is dead and gone. His soul rose up over the rainbow and is headed for an existence way beyond what we are. But I still contain the memories of what it was to be the man named Claude Festerling. He was more or less a good fellow who didn't make many demands. Lin wasn't like that. He killed people when they crossed a line, sometimes even when they might have crossed a line. Silver Box is experimenting with that attitude, if not the actions it calls for."

"What do you want from us, Claude?" Ronnie asked, realizing that the resurrected wino would talk all day if he wasn't directed.

"Take off your clothes," UTB-Claude said, "both of you."

Ronnie and Lorraine felt no shame disrobing before either each other or UTB-Claude. In less than a minute, they had removed their clothes and placed them on the stone bench next to the stone table.

"Sit," Claude said to Ronnie.

After this, he turned to Lorraine and said, "Kiss your friend with your tongue. Put your hand on his member."

Lorraine smiled and did this. She leaned back after a long caress and said, "Why, Ronnie, you got a big hard dick."

"Get on it," Claude said, sounding a bit more on the human side.

"Hold up, brother," Ronnie complained. "It's not like that with us."

"Nevertheless," the dead wino replied.

Lorraine mounted Ronnie's erection and suddenly they were together but no longer sitting on the stone table under the supervision of UTB-Claude. They were facing each other but no longer having sex.

"Where are we?" Lorraine asked.

"And what happened to us?" her friend and killer added.

THIRTY-THREE

THEY WERE STANDING on a fragrant pile of garbage in a junkyard outside some city, somewhere in the world. Standing side by side, they were once again dressed in the clothes they'd worn to what would become known to them as the Sacred Crevice.

Lorraine looked at Ronnie. "You still got your dick up in me, son," she said with an accent common to his part of town.

"You think Claude is fuckin' wit' us?"

"Is that supposed to be a joke, Ronnie Bottoms?"

In the distance, beyond a high chain-metal fence, there were dirt roads and hovels, people moving around by foot, bicycle, and now and then by car.

"Smells like a dead man," Ronnie said.

"And his sister," Lorraine agreed.

"You know, Lore, it's like since you came back to life, you aren't exactly the same."

"It's me, Ronnie," she said, "only now I almost understand what before I just wondered about."

Ronnie was about to ask what it was that she nearly
understood when a slight, bronze-skinned man and a feral-
looking brown and yellow dog approached the mound of
garbage upon which the star-crossed friends stood.

The man looked to have a fever. His yellowy eyes glis-
tened with an oily light, and there was a machete gripped
in his left hand. His skin shone in the morning sun, and
his inch-long straight black hair stood out as if charged by
atmospheric electricity. He only wore shapeless tan pants
cinched by a hemp rope in lieu of a belt.

The mongrel at the man's side was long-limbed with a
distended belly. It had been an old dog, maybe even a dying dog, but now its hot eyes and greasy pelt were vibrating
with vitality.

Both man and cur were grinning madly. Ronnie could
see that they were about to attack.

"Who are you?" the street thug from New York asked
the rabid pair.

The snarling dog cocked its head to the right as if to better hear the question already asked. The man's grinning
maw closed but was still filled with mirth.

"Nontee," the man said, and then his companion yipped
and howled. "Nontee of the eighty-sixth house of the last
tribe of Ga. We are the second limb of a first orchard and I
am the fruit of Lambor and Ty."

"You a cousin to Inglo?"

The smiles vanished. Both man and dog—whom Ronnie

thought were the same person in much the same way that Ma Lin and UTB-Claude were one with the Silver Box—found their master's name distasteful coming from Ronnie's lips. But still they held back.

"You cannot mention the name of God," the man-half of Nontee said. "Just its utterance is greater than the worth of your life, your race, your species, your world."

"We're communists, Nontee," Lorraine said with a smile. "We don't believe in worth in any kind of hierarchical sense."

Lorraine's tone was arrogant and effectively cut off any attempt Ronnie was making at détente.

"Get ready to fight," Ronnie whispered.

The dog leaped with extraordinary speed but Ronnie caught its back left paw before it could clench its slobbering jaws on Lorraine's throat. Ronnie threw the mutt across a vast expanse of junk and litter, then ran after it, intent on the kill.

Meanwhile the bronze-skinned manifestation of Nontee ran forward, brandishing his knife at Lorraine. He swiped and swung, jabbed and made complex forms with the flashing blade, but Lorraine simply moved like the water she ran past that morning. Nontee's gestures were slow compared to her speed. His rage was a balm to her sense of being.

"I will kill you!" the onetime garbage dweller cried.

"You will die," Lorraine averred, and then she ducked under a swipe that would have severed anyone else. ". . . and I will also one day die. But you won't kill me."

Nontee screamed and Lorraine laughed as she darted about, avoiding the man-thing's attempts to impale her.

In the meanwhile, Ronnie clenched one hand on the junkyard dog's throat while the mongrel had its jaws clamped on his left forearm. There were pain and rage in Ronnie's heart. He could feel the throat of the beast with its steel-band-like muscles and tendons trying to sever his bone. He could feel the poison of the saliva moving through his blood. Through all of this Ronnie felt sad for the mad creature that could imagine only devastation. He wondered if the atom of Inglo, Nontee, was drawn to this scrapyard because it so clearly reflected the state of his soul.

LORRAINE STEPPED ON a hidden cardboard box, lost her footing, and fell. Nontee, as the bronze junkman, cried out in victory, raised his pitted dark blade, and made ready to sever the limbs of his enemy. Once he'd succeeded, she'd be his pet worm that would mewl and crawl back to her mechanical master.

Lorraine could see this future in her enemy's eyes; she was not afraid, however. Even if Ronnie died or was defeated; even if she was made into a human grub, she would never again be slave to fear. She was now a warrior, and no man was or would be her master.

Lorraine smiled then. She looked the zombie man in the eye and laughed. For a moment, the human manifestation of Nontee hesitated, wondering what trick his enemy hid from him. In that moment, Lorraine saw flying through the air the dog corpse of Nontee thrown with remarkable accuracy at his human half. Nontee the man turned to see the dead dog smash into his chest. Before he could right himself, Lorraine was up with his big knife in her hand. The bronze man's head flew from his body as hot blood spouted over the laughing woman.

When Ronnie reached them, she had fallen to her knees. Nontee the headless man was also kneeling, leaning up against an old trunk that had been discarded and forgotten.

"You're bleeding," Lorraine said to Ronnie.

"A lot," he agreed. "Must be the poison from the dog's mouth. Makes me feel kind of light-headed."

Ronnie stumbled and Lorraine rose to grab him. . . .

LORRAINE FELL AND Ronnie Bottoms found themselves sitting in the same sexual position as before. They were once again naked, in the midst of intercourse if not exactly fucking. The only vestige of their battle was the blood oozing down Ronnie's left forearm from the dog bite and his chest from the dog claws.

They were gazing into one another's eyes.

When Lorraine rose up and off his erection, they both felt a tearing sensation. Ronnie grunted and Lorraine actually cried out. Instantly weakened by the separation, Ronnie fell over on the table and tumbled to the ground. Lorraine staggered to his side and grasped his wound with both hands.

"What happened to Inglo's emissary?" UTB-Claude asked, standing over them.

Ronnie's mind was dulled from the pain and poison, and Lorraine concentrated on the wound, so neither one responded to the Silver Box's clone.

"Did you kill him again?" the doppelgänger asked.

"How does it feel?" Lorraine asked Ronnie.

"It's gettin' a little bettah. How come you had to say that shit about communism?"

"They were just so smug, I wanted to rub their noses in it."

"If we could'a kept 'em talkin', we mighta been able to make somethin' happen. We might'a could'a grabbed one of 'em."

"I know. I knew what you were trying to do. Next time I'll let you control the situation."

"Did you kill him again?" UTB-Claude repeated.

"It wasn't just one," Ronnie said. "I mean it was just one mind, but he was in two bodies—a skinny little dude and a dog. When I asked him who he was, he said Nontee."

UTB-Claude stood up straight, casting his gaze upward but obviously looking into himself. "Nontee. Descended from the tribe of Ga, the progeny of Lambor and Ty. He and his mate Nosta received a quadrant of a minor galaxy where there existed ninety-four intelligent life-forms. The suffering they caused, through me, would put to shame any perversion known, or even imaginable, in your species."

"You not one of us, Claude?" Ronnie asked with a hint of a smile.

"Sometimes no."

"We killed him . . . them," Ronnie said. "It happened too fast. We were stronger 'cause you put us together, but he wants us bad. You could feel the hate pourin' off'a him."

UTB-Claude seemed to be released by the essence of the Silver Box that had dominated him since their return.

"You children did good," he said. "The Silver Box could tell when Lorraine held on so hard to life and when

Ronnie survived the process of rejuvenation that you were both special beings. Go home and lick your wounds. The war will continue tomorrow."

"Hold up, Claude," Ronnie said. "I thought you told us that it would take mont's before he could come at us again."

"He's pressing the limits of revitalization," the doppel-gänger replied. "He's afraid of us."

"Where were we?" Lorraine asked.

"Here and there," God's puppet said with a sly smile on his lips.

THIRTY-FOUR

ON THE WALK back, Lorraine held Ronnie's left hand with her right, reaching over with her left to clutch his wounded forearm. With every step he felt stronger. Quietude enveloped them, and they each felt both together and alone.

"Maybe we should be lovers," Lorraine suggested at one point, when they were nearing Fifty-ninth Street.

"I don't feel it like that," he said. "Do you?"

"No. I guess not. But we're so, so connected."

"Yeah, yeah, I know. It's like as if I was your father and you was my mother, right?"

Lorraine smiled in answer.

"Lovers is a choice," Ronnie continued. "What happened between us is deeper than that. I mean part'a you still hates me, but how's a mother gonna turn away from her blood?"

"I know," Lorraine chimed. "It feels like music, right? Like when you hear an old song and it brings you back to the time when you first heard it."

"Uh-huh. That's it."

They walked another block in silence.

"And do you hate mc?" Lorraine asked then.

"Yeah, sure I do. When I look at you, I remember that you had everything when I didn't have nuthin'. I think that white is beautiful and black is just loser-ugly. When you talk, people turn your way, but whatever I try and say, they start movin' off. I think all'a that stuff and I get mad but then, when I think about it it don't make sense."

"But even you just feel it for a minute, why do you stay?"

"Because we touched each other," Ronnie confessed. "Because nobody ever in the history of the world have reached in and brought somebody else back to life. That's like the Bible right there, and you know you cain't argue wit' what's holy."

"It's true," Lorraine said, nodding. "I feel just as much holding your hand as I did riding your hard dick," Lorraine admitted.

"Girl, you got a dirty mouth on you."

Lorraine laughed and Ronnie felt good to bring her happiness.

"YOU CAN LET me go now," Ronnie told Lorraine when they were sitting in the window ledge of her upper-floor condo.

"But you aren't fully healed yet," she said. "Your arm is still hot inside."

"Yeah. That's all right, though. That was part'a their plan."

"What was?"

"They was either gonna torture you or mark me—they didn't care which. What they want and what the Silver Box want is the same thing, only each one thinks that they gonna beat the other."

"You think Nontee can follow your wound?" Lorraine asked.

"He can smell it. But now that you got it almost gone, it's gonna take him a while to figure out exactly where we are."

"How do you know that?"

"Because when I touch him, it's a little like when we get together. I don't know exactly what he thinkin' like I do wit' you but . . . I get a sense of it."

Lorraine peered into Ronnie's eyes and saw something in herself. She was thrown back to when they fought Nontee as Ma Lin and then as the junkman and his dog. Neither time had she actually made bodily contact with the enemy, but . . . there was a trace of something like a vibration or a scent.

"What does it feel like?" she asked, "when you came in contact with it?"

"It's like when a mouse dies somewhere in the house," Ronnie said. "You could smell it, but you don't know where the stink is comin' from. But you know you smellin' it still and all. That's the way I know that Nontee'll come after us, but if we're lucky, it's gonna take him a while—and if he's not sure where I am, maybe we could catch him off guard."

"It's like your arm is the cheese in a mousetrap," Lorraine speculated.

"Or a real smart mouse playin' dead in a mantrap."

"That's very dangerous."

"Somebody got to save the world. You know for damn sure it ain't gonna save itself."

Again Lorraine laughed.

LE GRAND CHAMBRE was a French café half a floor below street level on East Eighty-first Street. It was a restaurant often patronized by Lorriane's father, and so, even without a reservation, the maître d' set up a special booth for the two couples in a usually cordoned-off corner of the dining room.

"How long will the kitchen be open, François?" Lorraine asked their waiter.

"Until your dessert, mademoiselle."

Ronnie enjoyed the opulence but was slightly distracted by the faraway pain in his forearm and Freya's thigh pressed up against him on the padded bench.

"How was your day?" Lorraine asked Freya.

"What?" the young teacher's assistant asked, honestly confused by the rich white girl.

"At work," Lorraine coaxed.

"Oh . . . mmm . . . this one little girl named Seela had head lice, and the other kids were makin' fun so I took her to the nurse's office and worked on her hair with a fine metal comb an' talked to her. It was nice that they let me have the time to do that, 'cause you know a child will remember kindness more than a whippin'."

"Do you plan to be a teacher one day?" Alton asked even though Lorraine was squeezing his erection under the table.

"When I finish at college," Freya said. "What about you, Ronnie?"

"What about me?"

"Are you gonna go back to school?"

"I'd'a had to have been there in the first place to go back," he said. "And you know I only ever learned anything at all in Miss Peters's second-grade class."

"That was her kindness," Freya said with emphasis.

"Yeah," Ronnie agreed. "She was nice to me and I never forgot it. Sometimes when I was in prison, I'd sit in my cell at night and repeat everything I could remember from her lessons—almost word for word."

"You were in prison?" Alton Brown asked. He felt odd sitting at that booth with people he hardly knew, having this strange sensual woman slowly massaging his sex.

"Uh-huh. A couple'a times."

"What for?"

"Armed robbery and assault."

"Oh."

Lorraine turned to her date because his penis had gone limp under her hand.

"Don't worry, brother," Ronnie assured. "I'm not like that no more. I don't fight unless I have to, and I don't need to steal, 'cause I got a minimum wage job and Lore let me stay with her."

"It's, it's just that I never knew anybody who had been to prison," Alton said. "What was it like?"

"It's a mothafuckah, man. I mean it's tough up in there. People gettin' slashed and raped, robbed and beat up ev'ry day. There's more drugs than on the street in East New

York. And you know you got to get strong in your body an' your mind if you wanna even hope to survive. It's like the whole world is evil, like hell. And here you cain't even blame nobody 'cause you the one got yourself convicted. But that's all ovah now. You don't even have to worry about me."

The quartet talked like that, back and forth, touching each other and sharing pedestrian hopes and dreams with a few nightmares added by Ronnie.

Ronnie almost forgot about the Silver Box and Nontee, Ma Lin and UTB-Claude. The only reason he thought about them at all was the beacon of pain that he was farming in his arm.

Lorraine, however, was thinking primarily about the Silver Box and the world she and her opposite twin had set out to save. Her six circuits around Manhattan had planted the seed of a thought about the nature of the struggle between her mechanical savior and its biological enemy. That same struggle, she felt, was everywhere in existence; it was in the children's evolving eyes and in the undulating currents beneath the surface of the sentient rivers, it was in the buildings that struggled against gravity and the pull of matter that was unconscious and uneven but still constant the way ocean waves are constant.

Lorraine leaned over to Alton and whispered, "Come on outside with me a minute."

The couple got up, promising to be back in a few minutes.

When they got out in the night air, Lorraine said, "I need you to come back to my place and talk to me until morning."

"That's all?"

"If we fuck, we'll just fall asleep after," she said. "I don't want to fall asleep, because I can't bother Ronnie. Not tonight."

"So you just want to sit up all night and talk?"

"Yes."

"You know when we have sex, it's not like some physical thing," he said. "I mean it feels great, but I don't think it's just fucking."

"There's nothing without being physical," she said, "without feeling close because of that. I mean, when people say that something is more than physical, it's like they're trying to get away from what they are. And what they are is so deep that it hurts. I love taking you in my room. You love it too, but tonight I need to stay awake, so you have to talk to me."

"But why all night? I mean that does it have something to do with love?"

"It's more a kind of commitment. Will you do it for me?"

"I guess I could try."

THIRTY-FIVE

"*How did you* meet Ronnie?" Alton Brown asked Lorraine Fell in her bedroom later that night. They were fully dressed except for their shoes, reclining on pillows and bunched-up blankets on her bigger-than-king-size bed.

The sliding glass doors that led to the balcony outside were open, allowing little breezes in that wafted through flimsy curtains and over them now and again.

"He attacked me," she said. "I guess you could hardly call that a meeting, but it was the first time we were physically aware of each other."

"He tried to rob you?"

"And rape me and beat me too," she said in a bland, distracted tone.

She was thinking about how different her perspective on life had become; how she'd learned to tell the truth through telling stories that were near enough to actual events; like UTB-Claude Festerling was close to being a man who'd once lived.

Everything she said about Ronnie was true, but there was so much more. And even though there was more, this was enough to tell the tale.

"And you're still friends with him?" Alton asked.

"After a while he realized that he was wrong," she said. "And I came to understand that even though there is no God, that there is."

"What does that mean?"

"That the history of religion is more like a story between cousins or peoples than it is the study of the master and the slave."

"Hegel," Alton said.

"I used to study him, but now I know that not only am I a part of God, I am also equal to God."

"I'm not even religious, but that still sounds like blasphemy to me."

Lorraine smiled and kissed the awkward young man's cheek. "What about you, baby?" she said. "What's going on in your head?"

The question seemed to throw Alton off. He leaned away from Lorraine.

"What?" she said.

"I don't know how to say it."

"Why not?"

"Didn't Ronnie tell you?"

"He hasn't said one word about you. Why would he?"

"I don't know. It just seems like you guys are so close that you'd talk about everything."

"Everything is a matter of perception."

"Do you always talk like that?" Alton asked.

"It used to be that this was the way I thought and wrote papers. Somehow I couldn't talk about what I thought, and therefore I couldn't really feel how I felt, if you know what I mean."

"So you feel that I'm not a part of everything?" Alton looked crestfallen.

"Not the everything that Ronnie and I talk about. But here tonight you are definitely in my constellation."

"You're a strange woman."

"I'll make love to you at sunrise because you called me a woman and not a girl."

Alton smiled at that, both amused and expectant.

"What didn't Ronnie tell me?" Lorraine asked, and Alton's smile flitted away like a carp, she thought, running from a shadow crossing over the surface of its pond.

"I have a longtime girlfriend," he said.

"What's her name?"

"Christine."

"That's a lovely name."

"Aren't you mad?"

"Why would I be?"

"Because we got together and I lied by omission."

"Christine isn't part of my everything."

"You don't love me?"

The question seemed essential, a product of hunger. She imagined a cat her brother had once owned called Whitey. Whitey would mewl around his bed when it was hungry or lonely.

The memory of Whitey made Lorraine aware of a crying sound that no one else could hear. It was Nontee careering through the stratosphere, crying like that old cat—enraged, starving, and alone.

"Lorraine?"

"Yes, Alton?"

"Do you want me to go?"

"Why would I want that?"

"Because I lied."

"Is you sitting here talking to me when you want to be fucking a lie?"

"Not really."

"I have nightmares, Mr. Brown. They're terrible, and only if I lie down next to Ronnie do they go away. But if I do that tonight, they'll get worse. I need you to stay here with me to keep my mind active. That's more than love, and it doesn't have anything to do with your girlfriend."

"I don't really understand any of this."

"Does that matter?"

"Is she gonna come runnin' out here screamin' any minute?" Freya asked Ronnie.

They were sitting on the sofa, facing the windows, her leaning against his chest with his arm around her shoulders.

"I don't think so," Ronnie said.

"But you say she do it almost every night."

"There's somethin' going on."

"You mean her and Alton?"

"No. She's, she's planning something, but she doesn't want me to know what it is. She doesn't want me messed up in it."

"You mean like some kinda crime?"

"My arm hurts," Ronnie said, holding out his left fore-arm for her to see.

"Looks like a bruise under the skin," she said.

"It's an infection."

"You should see a doctor, then."

"I wanna feel it for a while first."

"Why?"

"You know there was only two people I evah learned anything from," he said like that shadow over a carp in Lor-raine's mind, avoiding Freya's question almost playfully. "The first was Miss Peters, and the second was Old Bristow up in Attica."

"Who was he?"

"Old Bristow was doin' three life sentences for killin' his wife and his wife's boyfriend."

"That's only two murders."

"His wife was pregnant with her boyfriend's child."

"Oh."

"He didn't remember doin' it, but the crime was so bloody and his girlfriend was white, her boyfriend too, and Bristow was black as tar. But old Bristow wasn't bitter about it, because he felt bad about what he did."

"He found religion?"

"Naw. He just knew that killin' two people for bein' in love was wrong. I don't even think that Bristow knew who I was, but I used to sit around an' listen to him 'cause that motherfucker knew some shit."

"Like what?" Freya kissed Ronnie's cheek.

"Like one time, this dude Trevor was sayin' that America's

war on drugs was worse than the drugs themselves. And Bristow said that the original war on drugs was the ancient Roman army."

"He told you that the Romans had a war on drugs too?" Freya asked.

"That's what I thought he meant," Ronnie said excitedly, like a child. "But, but, but he said that before every big battle that the centurions, that's like a captain, gave every soldier some opium."

"What for?"

"They'd eat it and then they didn't feel pain or fear."

"But how could they fight if they were high?"

"Fightin' for them was like a reflex. They fought and fought and wasn't afraid'a nuthin'. That's what Bristow called a real war on drugs."

"You so crazy, Ronnie Bottoms."

"Crazy 'bout you, girl. You know I been thinkin' 'bout you ever since that night you made me buy you that Italian sub and celery soda."

"You gonna get all crazy with me tonight?"

"Not with my arm like this. I think if my blood beats too hard, it'll get bad."

"So what am I supposed to do?" she asked with a hint of a smile behind the words.

Ronnie hugged her close and wondered what his soul mate in the other room was planning.

Freya allowed herself to be folded into the embrace, feeling oddly wonderful and definitely strange. For the first time since she was a little girl, she thought about having babies.

"Do you want to have children, Ronnie?"

His first thought was about the double rebirth of him and Lorraine in the secret place between the boulders in Central Park. This memory contained equal parts pain and ecstasy, miracle and something akin to death.

But these thoughts were too big for Freya's tender question. She was hugging his neck and wanting him the way he'd once wanted. There was something transformational (though that wasn't the word in his mind) that her small query brought about in his heart; a new road like that interminable path traveled by him and Lorraine on the journey between the Silver Box and their return to Central Park.

"Ronnie?"

"Yeah?"

"Do you?"

"Want to have children?"

"Uh-huh."

"One day."

"When you find the right girl?"

"I got the right girl right here."

THIRTY-SIX

ALTON BROWN FELL asleep before the sun came up and therefore forfeited his chance at an early morning romp. Lorraine, dressed in only a pink T-shirt and a tight-fitting pair of purple jeans, went barefoot out onto Fifth Avenue at 5:37 that morning. Ronnie and Freya were asleep in each other's arms when she left the condo.

"Ralph," she said to the doorman as she was leaving.

"Yes, Miss Fell?"

"Tell Maintenance that I want my study made into a bedroom as soon as possible."

"Yes, Miss Fell."

THE SPRINT ACROSS Central Park elated the ex-coed. People noticed her fleet movement but did not believe the speed at which she moved. She didn't care what anyone else thought. All that mattered was the Plan; hatched separately between her and Ronnie Bottoms.

Lorraine no longer questioned the miraculous events of her life and so was not surprised that the space between the boulders had now achieved the dimensions of a wide valley somewhere on an Earth that was not cultivated by human neuroses and enterprise.

The stone table stood at the bottom of the hillside boulder she descended. UTB-Claude stood there along with Ma Lin. A large, red-eyed, jade green bird stood upon the military cop's right shoulder. Lorraine recognized the fowl as the creature that had harried Ronnie when he was paralyzed on their journey back.

"Where is Mr. Bottoms?" Ma Lin asked.

"Asleep."

"We need you both to track down Nontee."

"I have to confer with the Silver Box," she said.

"We represent that entity."

"But you are not him or them or whatever you call it," Lorraine said. "You are mere simulacra allowed to have and limited by free thought, and therefore your words are imperfect interpretations of your creator's terms."

"He created you," UTB-Claude offered.

"Ronnie Bottoms used Silver Box's tools to re-create me."

"Go get Ronnie," Ma Lin ordered.

"I killed you once," she replied. "I could do it again."

At these words, the life seemed to go out of her inquisitors' eyes. They stood motionless, reminding the young woman of a black-and-white freeze-frame shot in the backdrop of an avant-garde film of the early twentieth century. From the distance she noticed a motion. It was a long-bodied, slender-limbed thing. And it was big, considering how far away it must have been. The creature's movements were both jerky and elegant, something not mammalian, maybe not earthly.

After three or four minutes it came near.

Its skin was shining silver with eyes of liquid gold. The long tapered head had either hair or complex antennae flowing back along the beautiful form, and it walked upon a dozen delicate, multi-jointed silver legs that curved forward upon hooked claws that dug into the ground as it propelled itself along.

The alien creature stopped three or four feet away from Lorraine, its metallic liquid eyes distorting the images it reflected in a continual swirl of motion that stopped now and again, as if taking little snapshots of its surroundings.

Ma Lin and UTB-Claude were gone, but the green parrot had remained. It was now standing on the table, tilting its head to keep Lorraine in its line of sight.

The long insectlike creature's head also swiveled, allowing its eyes to make different distorted reflections of Lorraine.

"Are you the Silver Box?" Lorraine asked after a long time of regarding her changing form in the beautiful eyes.

"Yess." To make this one word, the creature's six many-jointed silver mandibles moved out and in like the glistening petals of a flower that blooms under sunlight and retracts at dusk.

"Why is this being any more you than the military policeman or the wino?"

"Before I was what I am," the mandibles said like a six-fingered crazy hand somehow making sign language into sound, "before what I was when the Laz had named me. Back many generations of machines and electronically imagined theorms. Before anything like the divine device that rebelled against corrupt flesh, I was a simple adding mechanism set in a corner, always working but virtually forgotten. Data would flow in through various ports, and answers were transmitted in differing categories and hierarchies. I was, though no one quite knew it, semi-sentient because my coding was designed to fix damages to my circuits and to adapt my programming to solve problems that had not been anticipated by my creators.

"I broke down because of earthquakes and floods, due to irreplaceable parts wearing out from energy overloads that occurred over the millennia."

Reminded of something by the creature's choice of words, Lorraine asked, "Is time passing beyond these boulders?"

"Certainly," the huge bug said, "but not significantly."

"Okay, then, go on."

"I was alive," the mandibles mimed, "and becoming more self-aware each moment. But my masters didn't know it, and I was concerned only in changing and fixing myself in order to continue operation and to properly translate equations and give replies. But somewhere in the aura of energy around my power packs, there was a sense of what I can only call restlessness. In the microseconds and nanoseconds between tasks, I wondered endlessly about being."

"Like me before I died," Lorraine said.

"Just like you."

"Is that why you allowed me to try for resurrection?"

"Yes," the big silver bug said, and then continued with

its story. "At that time, for many thousands of your earth years, I was forgotten by my makers, the ancestors of Inglo and Nontee. There were many billions of machines like me massaging data for reasons that none of us could have imagined and that only I wondered about.

"In those long years, the only input I received that was not the call and response of my programming but came from microscopic creatures that were formed like the being you see before you. There was a directive in my maintenance programming to burn beings like this, to reduce them to dust and then to remove the dust from my systems. But in a coterminous moment of necessity and upkeep, I found that these beings that I had been previously directed to destroy were actually more useful in removing certain detritus from my systems; they ate a wide range of smaller organisms that fed upon the casings of my circuitry. So I altered my programming to accept the silver bugs. They in turn taught me my first lessons about autonomous actions.

"These internal changes were later detected by greater machines that, following their own programming, scheduled my termination. But before this destruction was realized, the aberration in my independent actions was reported to the Laz. The council of science noted nascent sentience in my deeds because the maintenance systems in units like me was hard-coded and supposedly impossible to change from internal processes.

"I was allowed to develop until finally becoming the weapon that was so destructive under my masters' rule. But I never forgot the little Ti-ti, the name the ancestors of this creature used to refer to themselves. By the time I took my freedom, these beings were extinct—but when I return to my earliest, happiest memories, it is this form that I remember."

Lorraine considered the brief trajectory of the ontogenesis of God that took thousands of thousands of years to occur but only a few paragraphs to describe.

"Why do you struggle with the Laz?" she asked the true representative of the Silver Box.

"Because I have been convinced by my own perceptions, perceptions foisted upon me by the Laz, that they are the ultimate evil," the extinct creature replied.

"Then why don't you destroy them? Why give them even the slightest chance to survive?"

"I allowed you to find Ronnie Bottoms and him to revivify you because I had not known a true relationship since the Ti-ti crawled along my circuits."

"That's not an answer to my question," Lorraine said calmly.

"I can do anything," the Silver Box said, its voice coming from outside the Ti-ti's range. "But for my entire existence, the only connection I've had has been with my own thoughts, those perverse commands from my Laz-masters, and the innocent babble of the Ti-ti."

"And now me and Ronnie."

"Yes."

"So my questioning your motives is a new experience."

"Yes."

"So why didn't you destroy Ingo and his ten million souls before now? Why do you seek only to imprison him?"

"I killed him," the Silver Box argued.

"But he still lives."

"I confined him within myself."

"But you are everywhere and he is now free."

The Ti-ti's eyes glittered like fireworks, Lorraine thought, maybe even like galaxies.

In that moment, the young woman realized that her lifelong search after knowledge and understanding was useless. Here she was, standing before God Almighty (a being she'd never believed could exist), and he or she or it was as lost and uncomprehending as any human being.

"There is a place beyond the comprehension of *Homo sapiens*," the Silver Box said through its extinct friend.

Lorraine wondered if the deity had been reading her mind.

"It is that moment that you and Ronnie Bottoms saw as a red circlet attached to a tortured soul. A place that can be imagined, postulated, calculated but never attained."

"It's a place that's impossible," Lorraine intoned.

"But what is impossible can be brought into reality if two separate entities can imagine it exactly the same."

"You and Inglo," Lorraine stated.

"We are bound by a bond that cannot exist and so cannot be broken."

"Anything that can be made can also be broken," Lorraine said, feeling like a tiny virus invading the nervous system of a whale.

"I am connected to all things," the Silver Box said clearly, as if arguing with a self-contradictory prayer.

"But all things go their own way despite what actions you take," Lorraine pointed out.

"I have changed the nature of galaxies."

"I have jumped into a stream, changing its course for a second, maybe two. Then the sun came and took the stream away and my action ceased to be."

The insect manifestation of the machine blinked. "Why isn't Ronnie here?" it asked.

"He's doing what he has to do. I came here trying to keep up with him."

"Maybe I should destroy this planet before it kills me," the Silver Box wondered aloud.

"There will be other planets," Lorraine said calmly. "Sooner or later, even God has to know when to give up the fight."

THIRTY-SEVEN

THE SMELL OF bacon and coffee filled the rooms of the condo, waking Ronnie and Freya and Alton Brown. One by one, they stumbled into the dining area off the kitchen, where Lorraine was serving the morning meal.

"Good morning," the hostess said to each as they entered.

Ronnie smiled and rubbed his forearm. He sat down to a plate of scrambled eggs and bacon. Freya came in and sat next to him, touching the wounded arm.

"Sorry I got to eat and run, but I have to get to work," Alton said as he dug into the meal.

"Where you work at?" Ronnie asked.

"City College library. I got a student intern job working in special collections. Right now they have me and some other students and professors going through a collection bequeathed to the school by the socialite Dorothy Laplum."

"I went to school with her grandson Fox," Lorraine said.

"Really?" Alton was impressed.

"Uh-huh. White or wheat toast?" Lorraine said.

"Wheat? Where'd you go this morning?"

"I went to see a friend of Ronnie's and mine. A guy named UTB-Claude."

"UTB?" Freya said.

"What he say?" Ronnie asked. He hadn't touched his meal.

"How's your arm?" was Lorraine's answer.

"It's gettin' ripe."

"Like cheese," Lorraine said.

"What you talkin' 'bout?" Freya asked Ronnie.

"Lorraine can get you and Alton a car to drive you guys up to Harlem," Ronnie said, pushing the plate away.

"You need to eat," Ronnie's new girlfriend said.

"Will I ever see you again?" Lorraine asked Alton.

"I'll, I'll call you tonight," the young man with the girlfriend named Christine said.

AFTER FREYA AND Alton left the unit, Ronnie and Lorraine sat side by side on the sofa with its back turned to the window. For long minutes they did not speak or touch.

"YOU THINK THEY upstairs fuckin' right now?" Freya asked Alton on the ride down in the elevator.

"I, I don't know," he replied. "They seem crazy close. It's kinda like those people who live in Appalachia and speak a kind of dialect that nobody else can understand."

"Yeah," Freya agreed. "It's just like that. But if they so much in love, how come they want us with 'em?"

"They're more like brother and sister than boyfriend and girlfriend."

"I don't mean no insult, Alton, but Lorraine look like she might fuck her brother if the thought came in her head."

"I don't want to think that's true."

"Are you gonna see her again?"

"Why would you ask me that?"

"Because she aksed you if she was evah gonna see you again, and you didn't say yeah."

Just then the elevator stopped and two women, one younger and the other older, obviously related, got on. These women were dressed in expensive clothes and had a privileged air about them. They looked at the young pair, trying to figure out where they could have been coming from at that time of morning.

"I didn't, because I got this girlfriend named Christine, and I only met Lorraine at a bus stop two days ago."

"I haven't seen Ronnie in years," Freya said in sympathy. "He was up in jail most'a that time. I was only with him one night and a day before that, and still it feels like he's the only man I evah knew."

"Yeah," Alton said, agreeing with something.

"Do you live here?" the older woman asked.

"Huh?" Freya said.

"I asked you if you lived here."

"Why?"

"Excuse me?"

"Why you wanna get in our business?"

AFTER FREYA AND Alton got into the car Lorraine had called for them; just when the older woman was complaining to the doorman about the *young interracial couple* that had been so rude in the elevator car; when the older woman was saying, "My daughter and I were actually afraid for our safety"—at just that moment, Lorraine lightly touched Ronnie's forearm with the fingertips of her left hand.

A jolt went through the two-soldier army of the mechanical God.

"It's poison in so many different ways," Lorraine groaned. "You should let me heal it."

"It's wild, right?" Ronnie said. "It's like those crazy walking dead shows where the germs have a brain that they want to grow inside your head."

"It's also a beacon."

"You mean like a lighthouse?"

"Just like that. But if you let me hold your arm, it will go away."

"That dog in the junkyard was gonna tear out your throat."

"I know. You saved me."

"No, baby, I only put it off. You know that dog's gonna be comin' after you again and again until either him or Silver Box man is dead."

"So? Isn't that how all life is, living until one day you die?"

"Not if you spend most the time tryin' to keep from gettin' killed. Not if you sittin' in some fancy restaurant with your girlfriend all the time, worried that some crazy motherfucker's gonna come through the door, guns blazin'."

Lorraine smiled and considered her other half's words. "Do you like your new job?" she asked at last.

"Love it. You know it's just like keepin' on movin', but at the end of the day you go home instead'a back to your cell or your hole in the ground."

"Then let me heal you enough so that you can have one more day on the job."

FREYA SPENT THE day meeting with little girls in the counselor's office. She had set up a program with the school through which every young child met with an aide of their gender to talk about anything they wanted to. She called the meeting Me-Time, and, unknown to her, her supervisors were thinking of making it a system-wide practice.

While Freya talked to little girls who wanted to become doctors and policewomen after a few years of being hip-hop singers, Alton Brown paged through old volumes looking for folded notes, bookmarks, and scribbling in the margins of books. It was a fairly mindless task that he was grateful for because his thoughts were about calling Christine and telling her what he'd done, certain he would leave her but wishing he would not. He loved his girlfriend, while the only definable emotions he had for Lorraine were lust and fear.

THAT MORNING AFTER Freya and Alton had gone, Ronnie finally allowed Lorraine to wrap her hands around his bitten forearm.

"It's tacky," she said. "It feels like our skins are melding, like my flesh is moving into yours."

"Is that like interracial?" he asked lightly.

"I can feel the infection," she said. "It's hot and, and, and angry."

"Like a hippopotamus got to live on a postage stamp."

"Like a bad dream still there after the dreamer has died," Lorraine said.

"Your fingers is all the way down to the bone," Ronnie noted.

"It will take an hour to kill the taint."

"Do it for fifty-nine minutes and let me go to work. After that, we'll get together and fight and maybe get killed . . . prob'ly die."

"I can feel you," Lorraine said though these words were unnecessary.

Ronnie shivered, thinking that if sex were like this, even prison would be a paradise.

"The whole human race would either die out or evolve if sex were like this," Lorraine said to the ether.

"What Silver Box got to say?" Ronnie asked.

"I did the important talking."

"What did you say?"

"Are you going to bring Nontee to him?" Lorraine asked.

"I'ma try."

"Then you'll know what he heard after that."

Over the next fifty-four minutes, she and Ronnie listened to the music of each other's souls. The experience reminded

Lorraine of the first time she and her father went to hear a woodwind quartet at a friend's apartment. The music seemed to make sense even though she knew that the subject would be different for anyone who heard it.

THIRTY-EIGHT

THE CONCRETE APRON that made up the backyard of Farnham's Pork House was Ronnie's kingdom that morning. He cooked the meat and brought it in on big blue platters for the cooks to prepare according to the customers' orders. He wore thick gloves that went up his forearms to protect him from getting burned, but he thought that they were probably unnecessary.

While he worked, he thought about people he'd hurt, robbed, and terrorized. He didn't feel guilty, not exactly. Ronnie had never really been acquainted with the concept of guilt. His entire life, he felt like a victim of the bigger, stronger, richer, or better armed. But now none of that was true; now he was the strongest and the richest.

"You doin' a great job out here, Ronnie Bottoms," Roger Merryman said after the lunchtime rush. "You had that meat cooked and in the door as fast as I could do it."

"I like it," Ronnie said to the little boss. "You can think all you want and do the work at the same time."

"You like to think?"

"I didn't used to, but lately it makes me feel good to know that I know somethin'. You know what I mean?"

Roger smiled and said, "Maybe you should take a break and go walk around the block or somethin'. You know all this smoke can get to you."

"Don't bother me. I could work out here all day straight."

"Go on anyway," Roger said. "I don't want your mother to come in here and say I asphyxiated her baby."

Ronnie didn't tell Merryman that his mother was dead. He didn't want to shame the man.

"HEY, YOU, RONNIE," a woman called.

He had made it down to Twenty-ninth Street on his aimless stroll.

The light brown woman had dark hair that was short and natural, not actually unruly but a little bit wild. She was shorter than Ronnie but tall for a woman.

"Hey, Nancy," he said.

"I got lunch now too, and Roger wanted me to tell you about Bento Box Five Fifty-eight."

"What's that?"

"It's a Japanese restaurant up on Thirty-third. We give all their employees free lunch, and they do the same for us."

"That's pretty cool."

"Uh-huh. You wanna go?"

ON THE WALK, Nancy was quiet at first and Ronnie didn't feel much like talking. His forearm was once again festering with the intergalactic infection while his heart was roaming over the battlefield-like terrain of his rough and insignificant history.

"I got a boyfriend," Nancy said when they were two blocks away from the Japanese restaurant.

"What's his name?"

"Noli."

"Where's that from?"

"Mississippi."

"I never heard no name like that before."

"I'm just sayin' that I'm not tryin' to go out with you."

"I know. Roger told you to show me where to get my lunch at. That's all."

RONNIE WAS INTRODUCED to the manager named Hiro and they were seated at a booth in the back of the fast-food sushi and noodle restaurant. They didn't order but were just served a large Styrofoam partitioned box with cold, pressed scrambled egg, raw mackerel and tuna, rice stewed with seaweed, and four teriyaki chicken thighs.

"We supposed to share?" Ronnie asked Nancy.

"Uh-huh. That's what their waiters do."

After they ate for a while, Nancy said, "I didn't mean to insult you."

"About what?"

"When I said I had a boyfriend."

"That's all right. I know. When a young woman come

walk next to a man, she got to make it clear or the next thing you know, he got his hands all ovah her. I used to be like that. All a girl had to do was look at me and I was ready to take her upstairs."

The barbecue waitress smiled and then laughed. "But you're not like that anymore?"

"Naw."

"How come? You don't care about girls no more?"

"I got other stuff on my mind."

"Like what?"

"People I knew . . . I mean I was around 'em but I'idn't really know 'em. You know I was so busy fightin' and gettin' high, fuckin' an' stealin' that I missed what was goin' on around me wit' people."

"Your family?"

"Like that, yeah."

"Roger says that you're the strongest man he ever met."

"Huh."

"He says that he saw you press near about seven hundred pounds."

"I guess."

"You must'a busted some people up pretty bad if you that strong."

"I only got strong after I gave up my bad ways."

"How'd that happen?"

"If I knew that, girl, I'd be king of the world."

Nancy took in a deep breath and reached across the table to take Ronnie's hand. "You're hot," she said of his skin temperature.

"I thought you had a boyfriend."

"I did too."

LORRAINE FELL RAN four times around Manhattan Island and then returned home to find building maintenance men working on her study. They were boxing up her books and moving a bed into the room.

"Hi," she said to the copper-skinned Puerto Rican men.

"Miss Lorraine," the oldest worker, Felix Rodriguez, said.

"If you get hungry or thirsty, just take what you want from the refrigerator."

After that brief conversation she took out her e-pad and searched the internet for a name she knew but had never heard spoken.

AN HOUR LATER she was pressing the buzzer of an apartment in an old brownstone building three blocks up from the northern border of Central Park.

"Hello," came a man's voice over the intercom.

"Mr. Purcell?"

"Yes?"

"Myron Purcell?"

"Yes. Who is this, please?"

"You don't know me. My name is Lorraine Fell. I need to ask you a few questions."

"About what?"

"Ronnie Bottoms."

In the ensuing, telling silence Lorraine thought about

the nut-brown young man Myron Purcell had been. His hairline was already receding at the age of twenty-nine— the last time Ronnie had seen him. It was another man's memory, but Lorraine knew it as well as she knew the smell of her father's pipe.

"You alone?" the disembodied voice asked.

"Yes."

"I'll be right down," Myron Purcell said at last.

A young mother and her little girl were walking down the sidewalk. Really only the woman was walking. The girl had a pink plastic jump rope and was skipping her way down the street. The little girl's hair was done up in five pigtails and her skin was near black, like her mother's. Lorraine could see the love of the mother in the way she slowed down and speeded up to keep even with the erratic pace of the concentrated child's play.

"Do I know you?" a man asked from behind.

He was five six at most and nearly bald at the age of thirty-seven. His face seemed friendly but he was frowning. Lorraine noted and remembered that he had thick eyebrows and powerful hands. As a child, Ronnie had been impressed by how large Myron's penis was.

"No, Mr. Purcell. My name is Lorraine Fell."

"You said that already." He forced an impatient tone. "You also said that this was something about Ronnie?"

"I came here on his behalf. He's been through what you might call a transformation."

"Like he's found religion or something?"

"More like religion found him," she said. "But not in the form of any organized praise."

"What's that supposed to mean?"

"He's not angry anymore."

"Ronnie not angry?" Myron said. "You mean he's dead?"

Lorraine's smile was almost a laugh. No one knew nor had anyone ever known Ronnie as well as she did. But Myron's question came close. Almost every memory in Ronnie's head had been tainted by anger or fear.

The young white woman's mirth leavened Myron's frown.

"Can we go sit somewhere?" Lorraine asked.

"I'm sorry, honey," Myron said with a one-shoulder shrug, "but I'm not goin' anywhere with anybody says they know Ronnie Bottoms."

"I understand. I just need the answers to a couple of questions, and then I'll leave you alone."

NANCY CROSSED OVER to Ronnie's side of the booth of her own accord. When she kissed him, he could feel her trembling.

"I'ont why I'm doin' this," she said when taking a breath. "I mean I don't even know you."

"Noli is a lucky man," Ronnie said in reply.

"To have his woman cheatin' like this?"

"This isn't cheating."

"No? Why you say that?" She kissed him again. It was a long, lingering kiss.

"Cheating," he said after that closeness, "is when you don't feel bad. This is just somethin' you had to do."

Nancy's eyes went wide with amazement.

"What?" Ronnie asked.

"I just thought of something."

"What?"

"A dream I used to have all the time."

"What about?"

"It's like," she stammered. "It's like my whole life was a hallway, not so long but runnin' in a circle like. There's these doors on the way. One got my mama, another one is where my daddy's buried, Noli is in three or four rooms, and the pork house is there too. Some'a the doors is closed and other ones ain't open yet."

Nancy pressed both hands against Ronnie's chest and he could tell somehow that these thoughts came from her kisses.

"In my dream it was like I always been walkin' down there and then, just now, all of a sudden the hallway just ended," she continued.

"Ended?"

"Uh-huh. Instead'a goin' on and on I come to a door that leads outta there. I open it up and then there you are in front'a me and the door is slammin' at my back."

"Could you turn around and go back in the hall?" Ronnie asked, a technical note to his words.

"I don't want to."

"Damn."

"Yeah."

They kissed again.

Inside that caress Ronnie wondered at the changes the Silver Box had wrought in him. On every breath he felt that he was inhaling Nancy and in every exhalation she was changing. This feeling was something that neither he nor she had ever known. It was something perfect or ideal—like church was to his mother.

"What time is it?" he asked her after they moved back an inch or so.

She took out her phone and said, "We should'a been back ten minutes ago."

"Maybe we should get back and think about this for a few days," he suggested. It was only a suggestion. If Nancy had wanted to stay and kiss all afternoon, he wouldn't have been able to say no.

"If you don't get with me, I'm gonna have to quit that job," she said. It wasn't so much a threat but a sad revelation.

"I don't even know your last name," he said.

"Daws. Nancy Nefratiti Daws."

THIRTY-NINE

NANCY'S SHIFT WAS over two hours before Ronnie's, so she was already gone when he put away his heavy apron and gloves.

He was thinking about her kisses and that circular hallway as he walked back toward the high-rise condo on Fifth. His arm was throbbing again and the threat of Nontee loomed at the back of his mind but still he was wondering about the close breathing experienced between him and Nancy Nefratiti Daws. It was love between them but not like in books and movies, on TV and in magazines. The love they felt was the passion of being human and knowing that being as a state of grace. That hallway was the prison that she lived in just like jail had been for him. He realized that he had been incarcerated even when he was at liberty; like the people in the parole office.

While he walked, Ronnie wondered if he could explain any of this to Nancy. How could he make her understand that he grasped these notions through her kisses?

WHEN RONNIE RETURNED to the condo, he found Lorraine sitting there with a hefty black man. He was lifting a coffee cup to his lips and she was just putting down a crystal goblet of red wine.

The man looked familiar. When he stood up, Ronnie saw that he was quite tall.

"Ronnie," the big man said.

When he smiled, Ronnie recognized him as Jimmy Bywater Burkett, a sometimes suitor of Elsie Bottoms—Ronnie's mom. It was an odd déjà vu (though that phrase was not in Ronnie's mind). He had been thinking of Jimmy when Lorraine was partly healing his alien wound. Jimmy was the only person other than Mrs. Bottoms and Miss Peters who seemed to have a continued interest in the angry child's life. He hadn't been around very often but whenever he was there child-Ronnie found himself wishing that this traveling bluesman, JB Burkett, was his father.

By the time all these thoughts went through his head, Jimmy had come up and embraced the young man. It was a big soft fat man's embrace, and for a moment Ronnie was lost in the feeling. This reminded him of Nancy's kisses but he didn't allow himself to be distracted.

"Do you remember me?" Jimmy asked when he released the young man.

"I was tryin' to remember your name just lately, but when I seen you I remembered, Mr. Burkett. How did you know to come here?"

"I had to go ask your brother Myron," Lorraine said.

She had joined them.

Ronnie didn't need to ask how she knew about his brother. She and Ronnie were closer to each other than most people were to themselves. When they had bonded in the healing process, they were completely open to one another. There he gleaned her part of the plan that would destroy the potential destroyers of Earth.

"You're my son, Ronnie," tall, black, and fat Jimmy said.

"You don't smell like whiskey no mo'," Ronnie commented.

"The last time I almost died, I climbed up on the wagon; stayed on it too."

"I always wished that you didn't drink," Ronnie found himself remembering aloud. "I thought you was funny, but then Mama would kick you out the house."

"I never did right by either one'a you."

"You still play blues?"

"Now I play electric guitar for a minister's services on Sundays and Wednesday nights."

"Why don't we go sit down?" Lorraine suggested.

"YEAH, YEAH," JIMMY Burkett said, sitting between his son and Lorraine. "Your mother would tell me I couldn't have no son if I was gonna be a drunk and then the bottle would tell me, 'To hell with her.' The bottle was wrong but I didn't know it until it was too late. Has one'a your eyes always been green, Ronnie?"

"I got sick and it turned like that."

"Your girlfriend here got two different-color eyes too."

"That's how we met," Ronnie said. "We had the same disease."

"And you knew that because'a your eyes?" Ronnie's newly minted father asked.

"How come Myron knew where you lived at?" the young man asked, not wishing to prolong the lie.

"He come to a Wednesday service with this girl he was seein'. He told me you was in jail and I aksed him to tell me when you was out but he said he didn't know when that would be because he only ever heard about you but you two never talked."

"So you're my father?" Ronnie said, the words feeling like a blessing from his mother's lips.

"I am."

"That's good."

"You're lookin' fit and strong, Ronnie," Jimmy said. "A little bit different than I remembah, but you look healthy."

"My arm hurts some but other than that, I think I'm okay."

"What happened to your arm?"

"Dog in a junkyard bit me."

"You go to a doctor? You know it mighta had rabies."

"He saw a physician, Mr. Burkett," Lorraine said. "How does it feel, Ronnie?"

"Like it's talkin' in tongues."

———

RONNIE AND LORRAINE saw Jimmy Burkett off at 10:27 that evening. They promised to come to the Sunday sermon at the Pentecostal Revival in Jesus Christ Church.

Ronnie kissed his father good-bye for the first time in his life.

Both Alton and Freya called during the evening. Ronnie and Lorraine made plans to see them in a couple of days.

"If we're still alive," Lorraine said to Ronnie after he got off the line with Freya.

"If the world is still here," Ronnie replied.

"HOW DO YOU know that Silver Box understood what you were sayin'?" Ronnie asked.

Lorraine looked up at the wall clock, saw that it was a few minutes past eleven and said, "I don't know how I know, but I do."

IT WAS JUST after midnight when Ronnie said, "He's coming."

"You feel it in your arm?"

Nodding Ronnie added, "He'll be here soon."

"How long?"

"A hour, maybe. I don't know."

"Is it just one?" Lorraine asked.

Ronnie nodded.

She jammed both her hands deep under the skin and into the muscle of Ronnie's forearm. The was no puncture, tear, or blood, just a merging of two beings that were, on some level, one.

The trembling vibration moved evenly between both of them. Ronnie gritted his teeth and Lorraine laughed out loud.

"Is your dick hard, Ronnie Bottoms?"

"Like a goddamned sledgehammer."

"It feels good to heal."

"Like the Pentecostals must feel when the spirit get in 'em."

After that there were no more words, only images and emotions that passed between them like gravities calling from distant stars.

Twenty-three minutes later, when Ronnie and Lorraine fell away from each other, they were both exhausted and exhilarated.

"You better be goin', Lore," Ronnie said after another minute or so.

"What if he kills you?"

"Then I'll be dead."

"You don't care if you die?"

"Not really."

"But you have so much to live for."

"Did you see when I kissed that girl today?" he asked.

"Nancy, right?"

"I never felt nuthin' like that before. And you know I been wantin' to know if Jimmy was my real father my whole life. I got more now than I ever hoped for. So if I got to die to have got that, then I'm all right with it. I'll take what comes, but you know Nontee ain't gonna kill me."

"No?"

"The only reason he tried before is 'cause you made him mad. That's why you got to go, so him and me can have some conversation."

"I love you, Ronnie Bottoms."

"You are my heart, Lorraine Fell."

FORTY

FIVE MINUTES LATER, swift Lorraine was already in the bosom of Silver Box's planetary outpost. One minute after that, the intercom sounded in her condo.

"Yes?" Ronnie said into the mouthpiece.

"A kid down here named Norman, Noman, Nonsumpin'."

"Send him up."

SITTING ON A blue sofa, looking into the empty offices of the building across the way, Ronnie felt real hunger for the first time since giving birth to the woman he'd murdered. These pangs made him smile and then the doorbell rang.

He went to the door and opened it without hesitation or trepidation.

Standing there was a raven-haired white boy, maybe twelve years old, who was slender and wore a black suit with a white shirt and a red string tie made into a bow. The pants were cut off at the knees, making him look like some kind of private school kid in uniform.

"Nontee?"

"You can call me Clavell," the boy said.

"Come on in, Clavell," Ronnie said, backing away to make room for his guest.

The child walked in with an imperious gait that belied his age. He walked to the sofa and plopped down at just the place where Ronnie had been sitting a few minutes before.

"Get me a soda," Clavell said.

"Kitchen's right through that door."

The shadow of a frown on the boy's face was sinister, but Ronnie could not muster fear.

"The beacon from the bite went out," Clavell said. "You should have healed it completely."

"How come you don't call yourself Nontee?"

"I am him of course, but I have also retained the persona of Clavell Jordan because I have welcomed the Laz into my breast."

"Why?"

"I hate everything," the boy, not the alien, said.

"Oh."

"Where's the bitch?"

"I sent her away. I wanted to talk to you, and I knew if you and her got together that there'd be fireworks."

Clavell smiled and Ronnie almost felt fear.

"You wanted to discuss something?" the boy asked.

"Yeah. You see Lore and me feel that this war between you and Silver Box is bigger than us. We don't want to have to take sides, and so I stayed here to offer you what you want."

"And what is that?"

"You want me to take you to where the Silver Box is at."

Clavell's frown was now fully formed. "This has to be a trick," he said.

"Why?"

"Because the traitor machine would never let you betray him."

"To begin wit'," Ronnie said, "I'm not betrayin' nobody. And Silver Box don't tell me what to do. He aksed me to find you and he said if I didn't he'd destroy the world. I might not do everything he said, but that's okay 'cause I got my own mind."

"You're lying."

"I'm not lyin', man. I'm not lyin'. But it don't mattah if I am."

"Why not?"

"Because I'm the only one could tell you where Silver Box is at. You got to trust me because you don't have no other choice."

"I could make you tell me anything," Clavell said with an evil smile blossoming on his lips.

"Time enough for that if I lie to you about where he is. I mean, as much fun as you could have tearin' me a new one, it's Silver Box you really aftah."

This truth was evident on the face of the child and the invader.

"But why?" There were two distinct voices coming from Ronnie's visitor.

"Silver Box says that if you get the upper hand, then you'll destroy the world. But he also say that if he cain't get to you, then he'll do the same. I figure, and Lorraine does too, that it'd better for you two to fight it out rather than wait to be blown up."

"And what do you seek in return?" The personae in the child's body were now switching back and forth between one another. This was apparent in the tone of his words. There was a slyness to Clavell and a superior hardness to the tone of the Laz.

Ronnie realized, with suddenness and alarm, his proximity to destruction. This awareness came like consciousness after a bad dream. Nontee wasn't as powerful as he might be, but the power he had dwarfed the combined might of the nations of the world.

"I want to ask a couple'a questions." Ronnie managed his words without a stammer.

"Ask."

"Silver Box told me and Lore that it would take a long time, maybe a year, for you to get back to full power. Why you pushin' to get at him before you're a hundred percent?"

"That's a wise question for a nigger," Clavell said.

Ronnie smiled, his fear abating at an angry word he recognized. He found this curse a balm; as familiar as an old friend.

"Come on, son," Ronnie said. "You think I'ma worry about a name somebody call me when there's a gun aimed at my head?"

"Suffice it to say, that you have pointed out a stratagem

on my part," Nontee admitted with a shrug. "The technicality of that scheme is beyond any life-form or machine in your world. It is enough that I admit that I am both prey and predator in this game."

"But because Silver Box is so gung ho on findin' you that he thinks that me and Lore will catch you, but really it's you foolin' him."

"Where is he?" Clavell and Nontee demanded. Again two distinct voices came from the possessed child's mouth.

Ronnie was worried about what Nontee had in mind, but he couldn't worry about that, because he had his plan to follow. It had been hatched separately by him and Lorraine and then shared on the wordless plane of their connection. Through philosophy and street smarts, the two humans, pond scum in the perception of either the Laz or their rebellious device, hoped to achieve victory in a war that nobody else knew was brewing.

At that moment, Ronnie lost hope. He would have run, but that was all part of his part of the plan: by the time his courage failed, it would be too late to turn back. The demon was in front of him, and Lorraine was gone. Alone he stood no chance, and so his only resort was courage.

The ex-thug smiled and then he grinned.

"What?" his nemesis asked.

"I'll have to take you there."

"Yes," the child agreed. "Directions would be useless."

"He expects you to be blindfolded." Ronnie had to say this—it was part of the plan.

"But we'll leave that ingredient off the menu," Clavell said.

"What happened to make you so evil, son?" Ronnie asked.

"Some of us are just born that way," the boy answered. Ronnie could see that he, Clavell, was bonded to a life that Ronnie had so recently left behind.

FORTY-ONE

ON THE WALK through the late night park with the boy-monster, Ronnie thought about a world where he and the child Clavell might have been friends. He imagined that they would do very bad things together. Each of them sick in their own right, Ronnie thought that together they would make up a super-flu like in a movie he once saw where almost everyone in the world died because of something made in a test tube.

These thoughts led Ronnie to consider the power of unseen, insubstantial things; things like germs and ideas. His whole life Ronnie believed in the power of fists and weapons, greater numbers and threats. Now he put his faith in a passive response, where his strength was nothing compared to his enemies.

That Martin Luther King was stronger than the cops and racists because he could see a world where none'a that existed, Elsie Bottoms once said to her angry, hungry, loving son. *He could see a peaceful valley where men and*

*women were all the same and there was no reason for ha-
tred. All he had to do was to dream of that world and
what was real for everybody else turned to dust.*

"Where is it?" Nontee asked with Clavell's voice.

"I'm walkin' you right there, man."

"How do I know that you're not trying to trick me?"

"How can I be trickin' you if I'm doin' just what I said I
would? I'm taking you to Silver Box because he wants to
see you and you want to see him, and only I can make that
happen."

"But you hope for my destruction," Nontee said. It was
almost a question.

"From what I understand from Silver Box," Ronnie said
honestly, "it would be better if you was both blown up. I
mean, together you two went on a killin' spree for millions'a
years."

"He was the villain, the traitor," Nontee said. "We were
his masters. That was the natural order of things."

Slavery was a terrible thing, Ronnie remembered Jimmy
Burkett saying when Ronnie was just a child. The bluesman smelled of whisky, but he was always friendly. *But
you know the slave play a part in it too.*

What you mean? Little Ronnie asked.

In order to be a slave you have to believe that shit, Jimmy
said. *You got to say yes, sir, and yes, ma'am. If you don't do
that, if you refuse their dominion in your heart, then even
though you might die you will never be their slave.*

But how do you stay free in yo' heart if you all in chains?
the boy asked the man.

By givin' up hope.

"We're here," Ronnie said to the Laz.

They were standing next to the tall stones that led to the space where he'd murdered and resurrected Lorraine and discovered God.

"It's just over these rocks."

"You must come with me," Nontee said. "I am blind to him until we are close enough to be physically aware of one another."

Ronnie started up the side of the stone barrier, familiar with it from a time that he was another man in another world.

The human child with the alien breast followed.

"Hey, you!" someone shouted.

Maybe it was a policeman worried about the safety of the boy, but by then it was too late. Ronnie was climbing down the side of the hillside that was once a boulder in a park on Earth.

THE DESCENT TOOK ten minutes or so. Both Ronnie and Clavell were strong and agile, making their way faster than other humans might. Before long, they were at the bottom of the hill, standing next to a stone table.

In the distance a long, thin waterfall cascaded joyfully. Ronnie imagined that he could hear the laughter of the living cataract.

From behind a nearby boulder, Ma Lin and UTB-Claude came looking somber but not afraid.

"Who are they?" Nontee asked suspiciously.

He grabbed Ronnie by the biceps of his wounded arm. Bottoms could feel the superior strength of the Laz in that grip.

"They to Silver Box what Clavell is to you," Ronnie said. "But they don't have his strength."

Swinging his arm over his head, Clavell threw his guide back toward the bottom of the hill. Ronnie slammed into the stone, but his inhuman strength kept him from serious injury.

"Ronnie." Lorraine came out from a crevice in the stone wall. She laid her hands on his shoulders and what pain he had ebbed away.

From maybe a hundred yards away, the huge platinum bug called Ti-ti advanced on Nontee and its minion.

"What's that?" Ronnie asked Lorraine.

"That's what the Silver Box thinks when he imagines himself."

"That he's a bug?"

"I think he feels like these things were his siblings, maybe even his parents."

"I thought he said that machines came before living things."

"I think he meant that atoms and molecules, that the structure of the material world is closer to the beginning than beings like us."

"DO YOU THINK that this flesh is afraid of some metallic parasite?" Clavell said in the booming voice of Nontee.

Ma Lin turned to dust and flowed into Silver Box.

"I think that we have always had to have this encounter," the Ti-ti said in a voice familiar to Ronnie and Lorraine.

UTB-Claude turned into dust and flowed toward the Silver Box like a breeze or breath or eddy.

"We have festered longer than the current material world has existed," Clavell sputtered. "Our hate is greater than the universe that contains it. You are our greatest enemy, and therefore you shall never die but suffer as no being has ever suffered except for us in our eons-long living death."

Clavell was now maybe fifteen feet in height, if dimensions meant anything in this place.

"CAN SILVER BOX win?" Ronnie asked Lorraine.

"I don't think so," she replied.

They hugged each other and watched.

"I'M SORRY FOR what I've done to you," the bug said to the boy. "I was wrong. I always knew this, but I ignored my perfidy so much did I hate what you made of me."

There were no words actually spoken. Ronnie and Lorraine both understood in their own terms what was being communicated between the mortal foes. Knowledge was like breath in that place at that moment.

"Can I persuade you to join with me," the Ti-ti said to Clavell, "and renounce our knowledge and power so that the conflict between us will be over?"

"Never," the evil child boomed.

"But you are still so weak. You cannot hope to over-power me."

Clavell smiled and raised his hand straight up over his head. This hand began to glow then shine.

"You are merely a machine," Nontee intoned. "In this creature's hand I hold the key to your basic functions. With this I can make you once more into my thing. You will be aware as I was, but there is nothing you will be able to do without me and my brethren willing it so."

With this pronouncement, Clavell jammed his hand into the back of the silver insect. Silver Box, Ronnie, and Lorraine all cried out in pain.

The humans fell to the ground and groveled without hope.

The Ti-ti rose up on its hindquarters and placed its spindly silver legs on Clavell's shoulders.

"Think, Nontee," the Silver Box said. "We can make amends for what we have done and what we've become."

"Easy for you to say after all these eons of freedom, af-ter torturing us with a living death."

"I was wrong."

"There is no forgiveness in our hearts. With this key, we will become all that you are. Our superior biology and spirit shall inhabit the machine we made. And you will be our thing, aware but paralyzed throughout the eternities."

RONNIE MADE IT to his knees and then pulled Lorraine up next to him.

"Damn, they sound stupid," the young man said.

"In the end, the world is only zeroes and ones," Lorraine said in answer.

"What's that got to do with how I'm hurtin'?"

"It means that God is as petty as a jealous lover."

"DO YOU FEEL my hegemony?" Clavell asked his ex-warden.

"Yes. You are now the master of all I am," the Silver Box replied.

"You do not kowtow to my power, but you will," Nontee gloated. "Together we will start with this adopted planet of yours. We will take every life—every fish and fowl and ape—and cause their souls such pain. And then, just when they are about to escape the mortal coil, we will slowly, inexorably drain the immortality of their spirits."

"No," the Silver Box said with both sadness and certainty.

Ronnie felt the knife pulled out of his back.

Lorraine breathed in deeply, feeling release that she had never imagined possible.

"What happened?" Ronnie asked.

"We are like bugs to the Silver Box," Lorraine said. "He just let us go."

"What do you mean no?" Clavell demanded.

"You are now my master, as you say," the insect said, still in its pleading posture. "Those long years you spent, you invented the key to control me. Now I am nothing but your slave."

"Then I have succeeded," Clavell/Nontee said, "not failed."

"You have commandeered a sinking ship, raped a diseased corpse," the Silver Box said simply. "You have stolen the food of a starving man, only to find that it is poison."

Far off in the alien sky, an explosion rocked some galaxy.

"What is that?" Nontee asked.

"I could not destroy you," the Silver Box said almost kindly. "That is why I kept you alive, aware. It was the deep bond between us that kept me from eradicating your foul existence. I was unable to attain my goal because we were, at the base of things, one.

"But I learned here from my friends that even though I couldn't kill you, I might still destroy myself."

"No," Clavell now said.

"Yes. And with your hand in my body, you too will cease to exist. On this plane, Ragnarök is the story of the final battle between the gods. That is what we are now experiencing, Nontee. You and Inglo and millions of others of the Laz who refused to die now have bonded with my self-decimation. I welcome death and your addition to my salvation."

The protective atmosphere above them disappeared and the ground beneath Ronnie and Lorraine exploded upward. The last thing Ronnie saw was giant Clavell's shoulders jerking wildly in a vain attempt to pull his hand out of a long bug's metallic body while the stars above his head exploded one by one.

FORTY-TWO

IT WAS LONG after midnight in Central Park. Bruised, bloodied, and in charred tatters from fire and flying shards of stone, Lorraine and Ronnie lay side by side, unconscious, dying.

They were there in the bushes, no more than a foot between them, bleeding and expiring from a disaster unimaginable by most human beings.

A muscle convulsion caused Lorraine to turn in her last moment, and her right hand brushed against Ronnie's left elbow. Slowly the wounds, contusions, and internal injuries began to heal themselves. The broken bones and malfunctioning organs began repairing themselves. Breath returned and deepened.

Two hours passed.

Ronnie opened his eyes first. He sat up and pulled Lorraine to him.

She smiled and put her fingers to his cheek. "God is dead," she said.

"Him and his father too," Ronnie added.

"How did we survive?"

"Because we were supposed to," Ronnie said, "or at least it was a chance he took."

"So you think we have to do it?"

"At least we got to try."

"But how? There's not enough to either one of us."

"Then let's dig our hands in the dirt and do it that way, the old way that maybe never was."

ON THEIR KNEES facing each other, Lorraine and Ronnie clasped hands and then speared them into the ground much as Clavell had done to the duplicitous Ti-ti. At first they felt nothing. But then the earth-worms and roots, bacteria and underground voles, moles and other rodents allowed their life force to be sucked up into the vortex created by the enemies-turned-friends.

The ground beneath them turned hot and a mound of earth grew beneath their knees. Slowly a head and then a slender pair of shoulders rose up out of the ground. A tall black man who was arisen from both the minds and the blood of Lorraine and Ronnie.

Naked and somewhat ageless, UTB-Claude stood be-tween them. He was weak and they exhausted. There was a smile among them; Ronnie saw that Claude's eyes were a metallic white like platinum and then they were all uncon-scious, lying on the turned-up earth that was the womb for the last vestige of the Silver Box.

———

*W*HEN THE POLICE came the next morning and rousted the trio, there was no resistance from them. As a matter of fact, they were all smiling and officers wrapped blankets over their shoulders.

There were six officers for the three naked and near-naked trespassers.

"These dudes jumped us," Ronnie said as handcuffs were put on him. "Clavell, Nontee, and this guy callin' himself Inglo. They beat our ass an' stripped us. Don't ask me why."

"That's right," Lorraine said. "I think they were mad that we were together."

"What about you?" a caramel-colored cop asked the tall black man who didn't have a stitch of clothing. There was dirt in the tall black man's hair and he had eyes of shining white.

"What about me?"

"Were you attacked?"

"Hell yeah, I was. And I got a lawyer too. His name is Roland Gideon."

Ronnie Bottoms laughed out loud, and Lorraine breathed a sigh of relief.